Best friend 678-944-0874

I'm Changing
Friendships, Drama, and Oh...The Comma!

A Starlet Reid Novel

Outskirts Press, Inc.
Denver, Colorado

This is a work of fiction. The events and characters described herein are imaginary and are not intended to refer to specific places or living persons. The opinions expressed in this manuscript are solely the opinions of the author and do not represent the opinions or thoughts of the publisher. The author has represented and warranted full ownership and/or legal right to publish all the materials in this book.

I'm Changing
Friendships, Drama, and Oh...The Comma!
All Rights Reserved.
Copyright © 2010 Starlet Reid
v4.0

Cover illustration by Kelly J. Browniee

This book may not be reproduced, transmitted, or stored in whole or in part by any means, including graphic, electronic, or mechanical without the express written consent of the publisher except in the case of brief quotations embodied in critical articles and reviews.

Outskirts Press, Inc.
http://www.outskirtspress.com

ISBN: 978-1-4327-4026-9

Library of Congress Control Number: 2010934125

Outskirts Press and the "OP" logo are trademarks belonging to Outskirts Press, Inc.

PRINTED IN THE UNITED STATES OF AMERICA

Chapter 1

"I can't fit them," Tina yelled from the fitting room.

"Let me see," her mother said, pulling the curtain back. She put her purse on the empty hook on the wall and closed the curtain.

"Mom, what are you doing?" an outraged Tina asked.

"I do not answer to you, you answer to me. Now let me fix these pants." She began to adjust the long pants that her eleven-year-old daughter wore.

Tina stood in her white tank and a pair of extremely tight pants. Her pants were so tight that her stomach hung over the waistband. School shopping was supposed to be fun and exciting, but Tina was agitated and annoyed.

Why did her mother have to see everything she tried on? She made her hop and jump in every pair of shoes she tried on. She made Tina pull her arms up to check the sleeves to every blouse. She even had to touch her toes when she tried on a skirt. Now she was inspecting the pants her daughter tried on.

"Mom, they're too long and too tight!" Tina complained. "Mom, stop!"

After her mother fixed her pants she turned Tina around to look in the long mirror. Tina quickly covered her cold bosoms with her hands.

"Put your hands down."

"Mom, the pants don't fit."

Her mother grabbed her by the arms and stood behind her. A blank stare appeared on her face—a stare that Tina didn't expect. "Yeah, they're too big, I mean they're too small."

"Why did you look at me like that?"

"Like what?"

"You gave a weird look. I just want to know why."

"I just didn't realize that you were so developed up there," her mother said, getting ready to walk out of the fitting room. "We're going over to the bra department next."

"Bras? I don't need a bra."

"You need more support," she said, looking at Tina's breasts, which stuck out through her tank.

"Put your clothes back on," she said, grabbing her purse from the hook. "Besides if you don't wear one your puppies will sag."

"Puppies mom? Like really?"

Tina unbuckled the pants. Her stomach quickly bulged out. "I can breathe again," Tina said smiling. She tried to pull the pants down, but they felt like they were glued to her skin. She asked her mother to help her.

Her mother put her purse on the ledge where the other pants lay. She tried to pull the zipper down. "Hold in your stomach."

Tina inhaled. Her mother yanked and yanked until the stuck zipper came down. Tina's stomach quickly bulged out. "There you go," she said.

"Could you help me pull my pants off?"

"Come on now!" her mother protested.

"Mommmmm," Tina whined.

Her mother pulled at the waistband. ""Wow, these are tight," she said. "Here, sit down while I pull."

Tina sat on the ledge while her mother pulled. She watched as her mother's veins popped on top of her forehead.

"Are you guys okay in there?" the salesclerk asked.

"Yeah, we're fine," Tina said, breathing heavily.

"Let me know if you need me," the clerk said.

Tina's mother was very focused on getting the pants off. The veins on her forehead looked like miniature lightning bolts. She bit her bottom lip as she squatted ... then finally with one forced yank she got the pants off. "WHOAAA!!!!" Her mother fell back knocking down the fitting room curtain.

"OH MY GOODNESS, GET UP MOMMA!"

Tina could feel a cool breeze entering the fitting room; not only did her mother get her pants off, but her panties came off as well. The sales clerk quickly picked up the curtain & apologized. A lady helped Tina's mother stand up. Tina quickly crossed her legs and pulled her tank to cover her private area; unfortunately when she did this her breasts hung out. Staggered by the fall and her daughter's newly developed areas, her mother brushed her hand softly through her hair and adjusted her clothes. She picked up the jeans and removed Tina's panties from the pants, that's when she noticed the lady that helped her. It was Mrs. Simmons, Tina's new sixth grade teacher. "Hello, Mrs. Simmons."

The lady looked at Tina's mother, trying to recall where she knew the woman from. "That's right Krystina Morten. We met during Open House

I'M CHANGING

last week," she said, smiling. "You're Tina's mother, right? How is she? Is she ready for the big day?"

"Why don't you ask her yourself," Krystina said, giving Mrs. Simmons a clear view of her daughter sitting in the fitting room. "Say hi to your new teacher, Tina."

Tina was numb; she didn't even blink. This was a dream, no, a nightmare. *Please tell me that I'm not sitting in a fitting room, nearly butt naked and my future sixth grade homeroom teacher just said hi. This is not real, this is not real, this cannot be real.*

"Fix your tank, baby," her mother said, trying to whisper. "Oh, and put your undies on too," she said, throwing the panties at her daughter. Regrettably Tina couldn't catch and the panties landed on her head.

"Oh my God, I can't believe this," Tina said, crying. She snatched the panties off her head. "Mom, close the curtain. Oh my goodness, I am so embarrassed."

"Like you have something we don't, *girl please*," her mother said, closing the curtain. She could hear her daughter crying on the other side of the curtain. "That's my drama queen for you," she said, smiling at Mrs. Simmons.

Tina slowly put her clothes on with an attitude. She wiped her eyes and took a deep breath. She was ready to go home. Once she was dressed she started to pick at her nails. There was no way she was leaving that fitting room. The conversation between her mother and new teacher continued. *What the heck are they still talking about?* Tina asked herself.

"I know you have your clothes on by now," her mother said through the curtain. "Get out here."

Tina finally walked out of the fitting room with a major attitude.

"Doing some fall shopping I see," Mrs. Simmons said, smiling at Tina. Mrs. Simmons had caramel skin. Her hair was pinned in a ball. She had on a pair of jeans and a white blouse.

Tina smiled back, and then turned her head.

"Mrs. Simmons is talking to you," her mother said in that you better show your manners voice.

Tina forced a hello to her future teacher.

"They grow up so fast," her mother said. "Actually we're headed to the bra department."

"Mom!"

"Well, I look forward to having you in my class. It was great talking to you, Krystina. You guys have fun," Mrs. Simmons said, walking away.

"Time for my baby to get her first bra," her mother said, kissing her on the forehead.

"Mom! Kissing me in public?"

I'M CHANGING

Her mother grabbed her and gave her a bear hug. Tina slowly pushed her mother off of her. *How embarrassing, and Mom didn't even apologize for throwing my panties at me,* Tina thought. *Did Momma actually think I was gonna have a long conversation with Mrs. Simmons? Yeah, right! I can't believe she told her that I'm shopping for bras, and then she has the nerve to kiss and hug me like nothing ever happened.* Tina was mad and she wanted to go home.

As they walked over to the bra department, Tina pouted. Her tank tops supported her quite well, but she had to admit she was getting bigger on top. She glanced at the pretty bras on the racks and then she immediately began to smile. "I like this one," she said, holding up a leopard-print bra.

"I don't think so. Turn around," her mother said, putting a bra cup against one of her breast.

"Mom!" an irate Tina said. "People are watching."

"No one is thinking about you. Go try this on and these," she said, giving her at least five bras.

"What about the leopard one?"

"No!"

Tina made her infamous growling sound, but her mother ignored her. Moments later Tina walked out the fitting room carrying the bras.

"Excuse me, but I want to see how they fit."

"They didn't, all except this one," Tina said, holding up a white bra.

"Go back to the fitting room and let me see."

"Mom, it fits."

"I need to make sure."

"But I'm telling you it fits. You act as if I'm lying."

"What did I just say?"

Tina sighed and went back in the fitting room.

Her mother waited a few minutes. "Do you have it on?"

"Yes," Tina pouted.

Her mother walked in the fitting room and put her cold hands on Tina's back.

"Ewwwww, what are you doing?" Tina squirmed

"I'm checking the band to make sure it's not too tight."

"Your hands are cold."

"Stop complaining." She then pressed her hands against Tina's bra cups.

"Oh my goodness!"

"Oh your goodness what?"

"You're feeling all over me," Tina said, frowning.

"Get over yourself." Her mother looked at the tag. "Yeah, it fits, so you're a 32B," she said, reading the tag.

"Is that good?"

"How did you go this long without wearing a bra?"

"I don't know," Tina defensively said. "I told you it fits."

"All bras run differently. A 32B may fit too big or too small; it all depends on the brand. I need to find you a few more bras to try on. I'll be right back." Her mother stopped, then looked at Tina's butt.

"What?" Tina said, making her eyes big.

"You need some new underwear too," she said walking out.

Tina frowned, then poked out her lips. She looked at her reflection in the mirror. She couldn't believe that she was wearing a bra. She put her hands on her hips and turned in the mirror. She jumped, and then did a few dance moves. She felt comfortable in her bra. Suddenly she stopped moving, sorrow quickly overcame her. Marci was supposed to be there with her, going school shopping and trying on bras. It finally hit her Marci wasn't coming back.

Chapter 2

Tina was extremely nervous as she sat in the backseat of her father's car. The beginning of the school year always made her nervous. Starting middle school was a big step and she had many decisions to make. What was her style going to be? How was she going to wear her hair? Was she going to carry a book bag or a big folder with a famous cartoon character on it? Who would her locker partner be? Where was she going to sit? Who would sit next to her? It wasn't as if Tina didn't have friends, she just didn't have her best one.

Tina and Marci were inseparable. Whenever you saw one, there was always the other, but not anymore. Tina couldn't believe that Marci was now best friends with her archrival and next-door neighbor, Nancy Pepperdine. *Pepperstank* is what she nicknamed Nancy.

I'M CHANGING

Nancy Octavia Pepperdine was the thorn in Tina's side. They'd known each other since preschool. Nancy always had to have things her way and Tina was no pushover. According to Tina, Nancy was a total showoff and exaggerated the truth far too often. Like the time she claimed she had an indoor swimming pool with a diving board. The truth of the matter was the only indoor swimming pool that Nancy had in her house belonged to her dolls. When Tina confronted her, Nancy told Tina that she must have her confused with someone else, and that's when Tina realized Nancy wasn't just a liar, but crazy as well.

Tina had major issues with Nancy, but it didn't compare to the animosity that Marci and Nancy shared. In elementary Marci and Nancy were like oil and water; they just didn't mix. Nancy spread the rumor that Marci only took a shower once a week, that rumor stuck with Marci throughout third grade. She was known as the girl who hated soap and water. She even told people that because Marci was Asian, she ate cats. Marci was very upset by that negative stereotype. Tina remembered the arguments they had last year. They would argue for hours, screaming and shouting. Their arguments were so bad that the teachers had to keep them separated.

Tina remembered the time Nancy deliberately sat in Marci's favorite seat in the cafeteria. When Marci told her to get up, Nancy stood up, then picked up her tray of food and poured her lunch on Marci. Marci was drenched with fruit cobbler and chocolate milk. They began to fight. Marci held Nancy in a headlock while Nancy's arms waved for survival. They were both held in detention for one week. Those were the good old days that Tina missed.

Everything was changing in Tina's life and she didn't like that one bit. It all started last summer when Tina and Marci were playing with their dolls in Tina's backyard. Nancy opened the back gate and sat right beside them as if she were invited. Tina rolled her eyes because whenever she came over she only wanted to brag about something.

"Hello, girls," Nancy said, smiling. Before they could respond Nancy interjected, "Guess what?"

"I'm dying to know," Tina sarcastically said looking into Nancy's excited eyes.

Nancy lifted her yellow sundress over her face. Tina and Marci gasped in amazement as they stared at Nancy's black bra with a red rose in the center. Tina couldn't help but notice that her naval poked out. Little Miss Pepperstank had an outty, she said to herself.

I'M CHANGING

"You wear a bra?" Marci asked.

Nancy put her dress down. "Not just any bra Marci, but a black lace one, and not just any lace bra—the lace from this bra was imported from Italy. You girls wouldn't be familiar with Chantilly lace, so there's no need for me to go on," Nancy said, standing up.

"You really don't have anything to put in that bra," Tina said.

"I have so many things that you wish you had, Tina; cheerleading trophies, my picture in the paper, my own bedroom, frequent flyer miles, and a lace bra just to name a few." Nancy said. "I'll let you girls get back to playing with your dolls. I'm about to polish my nails. My manicurist is out of town, so this is going to be an adventure."

"Can I come?" Marci asked.

Tina looked at Marci in surprise.

"Sure you can," Nancy said, smiling at Marci.

"Come on, Tina," Marci said.

Tina immediately crossed her arms and frowned. They looked at her, waiting for a response.

"I think playing with dolls is more important to Tina than enhancing her appearance," Nancy said, grabbing Marci by the arm.

Marci shrugged her shoulders as she walked away with Nancy. Tina believed that if Marci wanted to get away from Pepperstank's clutches she could have, but she didn't. *Marci just took her old-fashioned, boney self next door!* Tina told herself. She was livid just remembering how she lost her friend. As Marci and Nancy grew closer, the further Marci and Tina drifted apart. Tina couldn't believe how quickly Marci changed. She started to wear lip gloss and carry a purse.

Before Nancy entered the picture Tina began to notice changes in Marci. They argued more than ever, but despite her change, Marci was still her best friend or so she thought. She wanted to cry when she thought about all the important events Marci missed, like getting her first bra. Marci didn't know that she finished writing her short story, *Cheerleaders*. Marci didn't know that she caught her sister hugging an 11th grader! She wanted to call Marci and tell her about the day her puppy Jerry humped her leg, but she didn't. How could she just drop me like a hot potato? All of our sleepovers, trips, fart and belching contests—how could she throw our friendship away and how could she be best buds with Pepperstank?

"We're here," Tina's father said, stopping in front of her new middle school. Tina stared at the big building; her heart felt like it was pounding out of her chest. The time had finally arrived. She never thought the day would actually come when she'd start junior high.

"Okay, Scooterbug, let's get you settled in," Tina's dad said, unfastening his seat belt. "Are you okay?"

"Just a little nervous."

"A little? It looks like you're going to pass out. Don't worry, Scooterbug, many of your friends are here."

"But not the most important one."

"Huh? I didn't hear you."

"Never mind."

Tina usually took the bus, but on the first day of school one of her parents always dropped her off and picked her up at the end of the day. Tina and her father walked to the front entrance of the school. She could smell the pine on the freshly mopped floors. She watched other students walk down the hall. She heard the sound of someone pulling on an empty locker handle. Her head began to hurt, and she felt a headache coming on, or maybe it was just her nerves. They were greeted by a short, stubby man who introduced himself as the principal. She was too nervous to catch his name and she couldn't take her eyes off the few strands of hair on his shiny bald head. She set her book bag on the ground and bit her bottom lip. Her father continued to talk with the principal.

Tina looked down the hallway and noticed that the lockers were small compared to her huge lockers at Kellwagen Elementary. Where were the decorations? Where were the posters of bears and children holding balloons saying, Welcome to Linton Hall Middle School? Where was the hall monitor? Although Tina had made previous visits to Linton Hall for her sister Patrice's plays, they had only entered the building through the auditorium entrance on the side of the school.

"You look a lot like your sister Patrice," the principal said to Tina. "Room 204 is upstairs, but you know the drill. Mr. Morten, about getting your visitors pass from the office."

"Daddy, I can go upstairs alone if that's okay with you," Tina said.

"But I just wanted—"

"Daddy," Tina interrupted. "You met my homeroom teacher at Open House last week."

"Are you sure?"

"Yes, it's time that I started doing stuff on my own," Tina pleaded.

I'M CHANGING

Tina's father took a deep breath and smiled at her. "You know, you're asking me to break a Morten family tradition."

"I know, but it will be alright. Let me go up those stairs alone." Tina smiled.

Tina's father hugged her and gave her a peck on the cheek.

"Okay, okay, I'm leaving," he said.

"I'll wait for you after school. Where *shall* we meet?" Tina said, changing her voice.

"Your mom didn't tell you? You're going to take the bus home today."

"Why?" Tina asked loudly. She knew that riding the bus meant being on the same school bus as Marci and Nancy.

"Put it this way, Scooterbug, we're both breaking a Morten family tradition today," he said, winking at her.

Tina watched her father walk to his car. She picked up her book bag and took a hard swallow; now she was on her own until she heard that voice.

"Why didn't your daddy walk you to your class?" It was Chante Baker, still wearing the same old hairstyle since the second grade. She stood in her usual funky stance with her hands on her hips.

Old nosey Chante Baker was back for another year of meddling in other people's business.

"Hi to you too," Tina said.

"Whatever, Morten, come on, let's go to class," Chante said.

"I'm waiting on someone," Tina lied.

"I know you're not waiting for Marci because she's already upstairs with Nancy, and they're dressed alike too. They look so cute. Remember when you and Marci used to dress alike? Ha!" Chante said, laughing as she walked down the hall.

Don't let her get the best of you, Tina told herself. Walking up those stairs meant entering a whole new world, a world without Marci. *Why did Chante Baker have to open her big fat mouth? Marci and I were supposed to be dressed like twins; that was our thing. Okay, I'll go upstairs with so much confidence they won't know what hit them.* Who was she fooling? She was a nervous wreck. How was she going to do this without losing her cool?

Chapter 3

Tina waited by the stairs for a few seconds then she slowly walked up the stairs carrying her notebook.

"Excuse me," a southern voice said from behind.

Tina turned around.

"I'm looking for room 204. Do you know where that is?"

Tina eyes brightened—a new girl!

"Hi, my name is Amanda Josephine Fields, but you can call me Amanda Jo." She tugged at her long blonde braid. She was a little taller than Tina.

"Hi, I'm Tina. I'm also looking for 204."

"Oh goody," Amanda Jo said, smiling. "I'm always so nervous on the first day. I just moved here. I'm from Nashville, Tennessee."

"I have family in the South. It's nice and warm there."

"It sure is. I miss the way the sun kissed my skin," Amanda Jo said, closing her eyes, reminiscing. "But life is like hair, you know, frizzy, curly, straight, kinky, and sometimes life is like a hairstyle twisted in braids, in pigtails, a scrunchy, up and down."

"Umm okay," Tina said looking at the new girl with uncertainty."

"It's the truth. You ready to find our new class?" Amanda Jo said, clutching her new folders tightly.

"I guess so," Tina said, adjusting her book bag on her shoulder. The girls made small talk as they walked up the stairs.

"Oh my goodness, this place is bodacious," Amanda Jo said, staring at the upstairs hallway.

Bodacious, what kind of person uses that word? Tina asked. She noticed classrooms 200, 201, 202, 203, and 204.

"Hot diggity dog, here it is," Amanda Jo said loudly.

Tina was quiet. There they were Nancy and Marci standing in the hall wearing matching outfits. There was an awkward exchange of stares; then the ladies walked over to greet them.

"Morten, it's good seeing you again," Nancy said, smiling. "You look exactly the same," she said, looking at Tina's breasts.

"I can't say the same for you—your stomach expanded."

Nancy smirked at her enemy. "I expected that kind of immature response from you, Morten. The old me would've talked about your kiddy book bag, and your cute little cubic zirconium studs in your ears, but Marci has shown me that pettiness doesn't matter. Gotta love a best friend."

"I like your hair like that, Tina," Marci said smiling.

"Fly a kite toothpick," Tina said rolling her eyes.

"Maybe we will, right, Marci?"

"Snap!" Chante said leaning against a locker.

Amanda Jo waved her hand good-bye and quickly followed Tina to their new class. Mrs. Simmons stood by her desk.

"Mrs. Simmons!" Tina said.

"Hi Tina," her new teacher said, holding a black folder.

Tina totally forgot about Mrs. Simmons seeing her nude at the department store. She was so focused on the first day and seeing Marci that she totally forgot about her encounter with her new teacher. She had flashbacks of sitting in the fitting room, covering herself, then seeing Mrs. Simmons' face. *She knows what I look like underneath.*

"Come on in," Mrs. Simmons said, smiling. "I'm sorry, I didn't get your name, young lady."

"I'm Amanda Jo. I just moved here from Tennessee."

"That's right, we did meet for Open House. Welcome to my class. Please have a seat." Mrs. Simmons winked at Tina.

Why did she wink at me? What's that all about? Tina asked herself. She took a deep breath concentrating on the empty desks in the front row. Amanda Jo followed right behind her.

"What's up, Tina?" Curtis Carpenter said. "Who is your friend?"

Everyone was staring at Tina and Amanda Jo. The same faces from last year filled the classroom.

"That's who you were waiting on?" Chante Baker asked. She wasn't even seated yet, but she already had questions. "What's her name? Why are sitting in the front row?"

"Trying to be the teacher's pet already," Louis McDougal said.

I'M CHANGING

"She's a pet alright," Curtis joked.

"Don't start, Curtis," Tina warned. "Don't start."

"What you gone' do?" Curtis said.

"Remember what she did last year in Mr. Greenberg's class?" Chante said.

"Okay, young people, let's start over." Mrs. Simmons closed the classroom door. "Last year was just that. You're in junior high school now."

Amanda Jo sat next to Tina. Could she possibly be her new best friend? *I hope she likes me. I hope I like her. What if she likes Marci? I'm not going to let that happen.*

Mrs. Simmons made each student stand up and introduce themselves. They also had to tell what they did over the summer. Tina concluded that teachers were just nosey. *Why do teachers make us do the same thing year after year? How would they like it if we asked them what they did over the summer? They probably took care of their gardens and shopped at the teacher store, a bunch of boring stuff, I'm sure. What makes them think we had so much fun? Shoot, we can't drive!*

"Since many of you already know each other from Kellwagen Elementary," Mrs. Simmons said, "Let's start with a new face. Amanda Jo, do you mind going first?"

Amanda Jo covered her mouth. She stood up and walked in front of the class. She smiled and said in her strong southern accent, "Hi y'all."

The students laughed.

"I'm Amanda Josephine Fields, but y'all can call me Amanda Jo. I just moved up here from Nashville, Tennessee, but I also lived in Alabama, Mississippi, and Macon, Georgia."

"You sound like my cousin Jesse," Chante Baker said. "He lives in Texas though."

"If y'all think I'm saying something weird or you don't understand me, just ask me what the heck I just said. We talk a little different in the South. We say soda, y'all say pop, just little stuff like that is different. Let me see, what else? I have a big brother and a baby sister. Anyway I like it up here in the North, but it's cold. Y'all fast-food restaurants don't serve biscuits and gravy or chicken biscuits."

"Like eww," Nancy said. "Sorry, Mrs. Simmons, but major calories." She frowned.

"It's good, girl, don't knock it if you ain't tried it. I had a good breakfast this morning. Momma made chicken and waffles."

"Eww," Nancy said.

"It's good, really it is." The class laughed, but Amanda Jo continued. "I'm a good student,

I'M CHANGING

never got nothing less than a B. I look forward to meeting all y'all one by one," she said, walking to her desk and sitting down.

"That's great, Amanda Jo. I just have one question, what brings your family here to Michigan out of all places?"

"The company branch that my daddy worked for in Nashville shut down, the headquarters is here so we had to relocate. Plus my Granny lives here and well, she's kinda sick. Momma tried to make me happy talking about I can make snow angels. I ain't never seen no snow before except on TV. I cried buckets of tears too when I found out we were moving. I miss all my friends; Jasper, Shelby Jean, Willie—Willie is so funny, y'all—Levi, Faith, Wyatt, Annabelle, Deacon, Lola Rose, Daisy, and my very best friend, Emma Grace."

"Why do I have the urge to listen to country music?" Curtis joked.

Amanda Jo didn't answer, but the look on her face made Curtis wipe the smirk off his face. Tina liked her spunk. After Amanda Jo spoke, her peers shared what they did over the summer. Although everyone had a boring summer, there was always one exception to the rule, and no matter how much Tina hated to admit it, it was Nancy who always had great summer adventures. Everyone looked forward to hearing her summer report.

Nancy always told stories about her exotic travels and adventures. Like the time she said the British government tried to hold her family hostage, or the time she said she helped train a wild lion in Sudan. Tina thought about the story Nancy told last year. Nancy said that while visiting South America her mother's purse was stolen. She said they had no money or identification. They tried to get help, but no one spoke English. Nancy said it began to rain like cats and dogs as they sought shelter. She said they came across a small village where people ate pig brains. The villagers painted their faces in white paint and red blood from the dead pig. The natives eventually helped them find their way back to the mainland roads. Tina had to admit that she loved that story.

Nancy stood up, brushing her long red hair off her shoulders. "Hello, my name is Nancy Pepperdine."

"Carrot Top," someone murmured. The class laughed.

"Like I was saying before I was so rudely interrupted, I'm an all A student—"

"And a geek," another voice said. The class laughed.

"Be quiet," Nancy said. "Over the summer I did so many cool things."

"Like what?" Mrs. Simmons asked.

"I'm so glad you asked. I went to Hawaii, Paris, Australia, and Japan," Nancy boasted.

"Dang gee," Chante Baker said.

"So who did you travel with?" Mrs. Simmons asked.

"Usually I travel with my mother; she's a photographer. My dad comes along if he can get off of work. I also went to Disneyworld with my new best friend, BFF, Marci," Nancy said, giggling. "See, we got this outfit in Florida," she said, putting her body next to Marci. "We're twins!"

Disneyworld! They went to Disneyworld? Tina could feel the prying eyes of Chante burning into the back of her head. Tina wanted to scream. *Pepperstank has gone too far. Who does she think she is trying to take my place?* She tapped her fingers on her desk. What was so special about Pepperstank? Was it the money, the designer clothes? I mean, really, her red stringy hair smelled like lemons and her breath smelled like stale potato chips.

Tina glanced at Marci. She couldn't believe that the girl she'd known since the third grade was no longer her best friend. *I cannot let her get to me*, Tina said to herself. *Just stop thinking about it and move on.*

"Mrs. Simmons, I have some disturbing news to share with you. Marci and I were once enemies," Nancy said.

"Is that right?" Mrs. Simmons said, sitting on her desk.

"Oh yeah," Louis McDougal interrupted. Louis told Mrs. Simmons all about what happened last year in PE when Marci pretended that her stomach was hurting. "Nancy kicked the dodge ball right in Marci's face." He laughed.

"Okay, Louis, enough of the interruptions," Nancy said.

"What a great lead in to our next topic, class rules and expectations," Mrs. Simmons said. "You can have a seat, Nancy. One thing I will not tolerate is rudeness, students talking over one another, interrupting others, and picking on others. Everyone, take out your notebooks."

Tina opened her notebook and began to copy the rules as Mrs. Simmons printed them on the board.

I'M CHANGING

"I don't know if I'm going to be able to follow these rules," Amanda Jo whispered to Tina.

"Just stick with me and you'll be okay," Tina whispered back.

Mrs. Simmons passed out the class schedules, student planners, and then she took attendance. "Okay, now I would like for you guys to count off one, two, one, two," Mrs. Simmons said. "I'm going to put you in groups. Once you're in your groups you need to pick a captain. I would like for you to discuss goals that you think are important to maintain a successful academic school year."

Students began to push their desk together; you could hear the classroom chatter as everyone found their groups.

Luck was not on Tina's side; she couldn't believe that she was in the same group as Amanda Jo, Nancy, Marci, Gordon Kowalski, and the mouth herself, Chante.

Chapter 4

"Isn't this special," Chante said, grabbing Tina and Marci's hand. "Reunited." Marci and Tina snatched their hands away.

"I don't want to be in the group with all these girls," Gordon complained. "I could understand if the girls were hot."

"Moving on, I think our topic should be—" Nancy said.

"Why do you get to be the boss?" Chante interrupted.

"Let her talk," Marci said.

"Mrs. Simmons said that people need to stop interrupting each other," Chante said.

"You interrupted me," Nancy said.

"You interrupted Gordon," Tina said.

"Sure did," Gordon said.

"Like I was saying," Chante continued, "Y'all rude."

I'M CHANGING

"What we need to do is appoint a leader and I appoint myself," Tina said.

"Where are you from again, Amanda Jo?" Nancy asked, changing the subject.

"Nashville."

"You really have a funny accent."

"You really have a funny face," Tina snapped.

"Mumph, guess she told you," Chante said.

"Buy any new dolls, Tina?" Nancy sniped.

"Buy any new combs for your hair?" Tina said. "Oops, I answered my own question," she said, looking at Nancy's hair, "NOT!"

"Bring out the Jell-O, it looks like there's going to be a cat fight over here," Gordon said, smiling.

Mrs. Simmons walked over to Tina's group. "There's a lot of talking going on over here. You guys must have some great ideas. I didn't know you were the only boy over here, Gordon," Mrs. Simmons said, putting her hand on Gordon's shoulder. "Maybe I should switch one of the girls up in exchange for a boy."

"That's okay, Mrs. Simmons, Chante is like one of the boys," Gordon joked.

Everyone, but Chante giggled.

"Okay, Gordon, I'm going to let that joke slip this time. Get to work please," Mrs. Simmons said, walking away.

"I'll be the captain," Amanda Jo volunteered. "If that's okay with y'all."

The group finally agreed.

"Before we go any further and since we're all together," Chante said, crossing her arms, "I want to know why y'all stopped being best friends. I'm talking to Marci and Tina, that is."

"None of your business, Chante Blabber," Nancy said. The table was quiet as everyone stared at each other.

"Man, you girls talk too much," Gordon complained. "Ain't that right, Chante?"

The first-day ritual continued with meeting the math, health, and social studies teachers. Tina and Amanda Jo stayed together throughout the day. Tina was so happy that she had a new friend. She was also relieved that she wouldn't be assigned a locker partner since Linton Hall had individual lockers. During last hour she looked at her watch. The dismissal bell was about to ring, but she had

I'M CHANGING

one more dilemma. Amanda Jo didn't ride the bus home, and that meant she had to face Marci and Nancy on her own.

Marci and Nancy were glued to the hip. They sat in the very last row on the bus talking. Tina sat next to seventh-grader Madison Bailey. She took a deep breath and looked out the window. The first day of school was better than Tina expected. She was very thankful that Amanda Jo was by her side. She still found it very hard to believe that Marci was no longer her best friend. Tina replayed past conversations in her head, but she just didn't understand what ended their friendship. Was it something she did or something she said?

The ladies arrived at their stop. Tina walked ahead of them. She tried to walk really fast. They talked about what happened in school that day. It was very uncomfortable hearing Marci's voice as she laughed and conversed with someone she used to hate.

"See you tomorrow," Marci said.

"See ya when I see ya," Tina snapped.

"How was the first day of school?" Tina's mom asked as she walked through the front door.

Tina closed the door, then threw her book bag across the room and went straight to the kitchen.

Her white puppy, Jerry, barked and scratched at her leg.

"Hey, Jerry," Tina said, petting the dog. Jerry was very excited. "Hey, move, Jerry, I'm hungry." The puppy continued to jump up at Tina. She tried to walk to the kitchen, but she ended up tripping over Jerry and fell to the floor.

"Are you okay?" her mother asked.

"Yeah, Jerry really missed me huh?" Tina said, getting up.

"How was your first day?" her mother said, following her to the kitchen.

"It was okay, too much stuff to remember," she said, opening up the snack cupboard. Tina grabbed a bag of chips and sat at the kitchen table.

"Tell me about your teachers, after you wash your hands." Her mother sat at the table.

Tina washed her hands and dried them with a paper towel. "You met everyone at Open House," she said, sitting down.

"That's not what I asked you."

"Sorry, I know you remember Mrs. Simmons, the one who saw me butt naked at the department store."

"She did not see you naked."

"Mom, I was sitting in the corner holding my boobs, and my panties were off—that sounds pretty butt naked to me!"

"You are too self absorbed. Mrs. Simmons is not thinking about you being naked. So how is she as a teacher?"

"She's okay. Guess what, Mom?" Tina said, eating her chips. "We have a new girl in our class named Amanda Jo, she's real cool. She just moved here."

"Where is she from?"

"Nashville, Tennessee and she's so country. When we walked upstairs she was like 'This place is so bodacious,'" she said, imitating Amanda Jo. "Oh and guess what, she called Marci a bean straw today." Tina laughed.

"That's not very nice and I can only hope you're not making up nicknames for people."

Tina was quiet. Her mother didn't know about the nicknames she created for Nancy (Pepperstank) and Marci (Shadow); she even coined Daniel Tucker's nickname (Inhale). Whenever Daniel stood next to someone, the students inhaled so they wouldn't smell his bad body odor.

"How do you like your new teachers?"

"These teachers are crazy."

"That's not nice."

"Sorry, but what do you call a teacher who gives homework on the first day of school? Middle school is going to be hard, that's all I'm saying."

"You can handle it. You're a good student who gets nothing but A's and B's, and this year will be no different."

"Mom, I got the feeling that this year is going to be really interesting," Tina said, crunching on her chips.

Chapter 5

As Tina entered her third week of school she thought about the three things that were making her life miserable; rules, studying, and homework. Just when she got used to something or learned something new the teachers were always switching things up and moving on to something else. "Here we go again," Tina said noticing that her health class looked different. The desks were pushed against the wall and the blue chairs were stacked near Ms. Hogan's desk. The center of the room had a big blue and red floor mat. Ms. Hogan directed the girls to walk inside, stack their book bags against the wall, and then sit in a big circle on the mat. The girls quickly did what was asked of them. Tina grabbed Amanda Jo by the arm so that she could sit next to her.

"God-ly, this is gonna be fun," Amanda Jo said, laughing.

That laugh was the only pet peeve Tina had toward Amanda Jo. Her laugh was so irritating—he-he-he-he-haw-he—there were always four *he's*, one *haw,* then another *he*.

The bell rang and Ms. Hogan closed the door. All of the whispers and giggles ended. Ms. Hogan was very tall. She wore no makeup. She wore her red hair slicked back in a ponytail. Tina liked looking at Ms. Hogan's pretty green eyes and light freckles that scattered across her face.

"You all may have noticed that the class has been rearranged. This year we're starting a new workshop in health that focuses on the self-esteem of our students. We wanted to start this program for our sixth graders who are transitioning from elementary school. As you may have noticed, the boys are not in this class; they're attending their own workshop with Mr. Carter's class down the hall."

Tina was certain that Ace Cryer didn't like this arrangement since he hung out with girls all the time.

"Once a week we'll meet separately, then we will have our combined health class on Thursday. After many discussions amongst students, teachers, and parents, we felt that students needed an outlet to express themselves about subjects like obesity, bullying, self-esteem, self-image, and other issues

I'M CHANGING

that may affect you. Being that I am the health teacher, we will certainly talk about what you're eating, exercising, and the changes your body will go through in junior high," she said, standing holding a notepad and pen. "You're sitting in a circle so that you can look at each other and express yourself."

The girls looked at each other and smiled. Nancy whispered something in Marci's ear. Tina was revved up—maybe health wasn't going to be so bad.

"Who are you?" Ms. Hogan asked as she looked into the puzzled eyes of her pupils. "I'm not talking about your first and last name, I know that, but who are you? What do you stand for, and how do you feel about yourself?"

Chante raised her hand.

"Yes," Ms. Hogan said.

"I'm Chante Dominique Baker and I feel good about myself."

"Do you let others influence your decisions?"

"Not at all."

"Do you give in to peer pressure?"

"Leaders don't allow that to happen," Chante said, fixing her hair.

"Do you think you're pretty?" Ms. Hogan asked.

"Heck-e-yeah," Chante confidentially said. "I'm fine."

The class laughed. She cut her eyes over to Nancy, anticipating a snide remark. She was ready for a potential battle, but Nancy just smiled.

"What if someone told you that you weren't pretty? What if someone constantly told you you're ugly or too fat?" Ms. Hogan asked.

Chante frowned; then she moved her head from side to side. "I wish somebody would tell me I'm too ugly or too fat; that would not be an issue, Ms. Hogan, *trust me*!"

Chante had a way with words. The class constantly laughed at her quick jabs and matter-of-fact way of approaching a situation. Tina couldn't help but admire her confidence. She didn't care if she had a best friend or not; she did her own thing.

"Very good, Chante," Ms. Hogan said, smiling. "I'm glad that you feel good about yourself, but it's a fact that many young girls don't feel the same way you do. Some girls think they're ugly, some think they're too fat or not smart."

"I don't understand why," Marci said. "You should feel good about yourself."

"That's true, Marci, but did you know a lot of young girls constantly compare themselves to other girls?" Ms. Hogan sat on the empty blue chair, completing the circle. "In this self-esteem

I'M CHANGING

workshop we're going to focus on making you feel good about yourself. We're going to work on some really cool projects, but most importantly we're going to share our feelings and concerns. We're going to talk about everything. Questions?"

Chante raised her hand. "Since I feel good about myself and all, can I go to Mr. Baylor's class and help the other sixth-grade class with their math?"

"No, but nice try Chante. This workshop will actually make you feel even better about yourself."

"I don't know if y'all ready for that," Chante said.

Hehehehehawhe. Tina tried to ignore Amanda Jo's laugh.

"Any other questions so far?" Ms. Hogan said, looking at the young ladies who sat in the circle. She nodded yes when she saw Marci's hand up.

"Will we talk about friendships?" Marci asked. "The reason why I'm asking is because some of us experience a lot of moodiness with our friends. Out of nowhere that person starts to act different; it's like they're not themselves anymore, like they're influenced by other people."

No she didn't, Tina said to herself, looking at her once upon a time best friend. *Why was Shadow talking about herself like that? I know she's not trying to say that I act different and that I'm influenced by other people while she's sitting up here looking like Pepperstank's twin for the third week in a row.*

"Sounds like a great topic to me," Ms. Hogan said, writing something down on her notepad.

"I just think that would be a great topic to discuss," Marci said, looking at Tina.

Tina and Marci stared at one another; it was the first time they gave extensive eye contact to one another. *If Shadow wanted to talk openly about how people influence other people, then she's going to get her feelings hurt, seriously.* Tina raised her hand and Ms. Hogan allowed her to speak. "I agree with Sh… Marci. Talking about friendships is an excellent idea because some girls don't know how to be themselves. They just like to copy off of others."

There were plenty of sounds out of Chante's mouth.

Ms. Hogan stood up. "Of course we're going to talk about friendships, but first we must talk about who we are as individuals, because once you have a strong sense of self, you will not let others influence you in a negative or compromising way. We will talk about issues and our problems, but this workshop will heavily focus on solutions and feeling good about ourselves."

"You're gonna tell us your problems too?" Chante eagerly asked.

I'M CHANGING

Ms. Hogan smiled at Chante and told the class that she will share some of her pre-teen experiences.

For homework the girls had to go through magazines and cut out beauty and body images of models and celebrities. The assignment was due that Friday. Tina was so excited—maybe health wasn't going to be so bad. As they walked out of class and into the crowded hallway, Amanda Jo immediately commented on the tension between Tina and Marci.

"She had a lot of nerve trying to talk about friends who act different," Amanda Jo said, holding her books. Chante quickly ran in front of them.

"Can I help you?" Tina asked.

"Y'all haven't learned anything, already gossiping *mumph, mumph, mumph,*" Chante said, shaking her head in disapproval. "What happened to sisterhood? What happened to sitting in the circle and having open communication? All this gossiping needs to end right now."

Ace Cryer fought his way through the hall and stood next to Chante. "Wait 'til I tell you what happened in our workshop," Ace said to Chante.

"Tell me!" Chante said, quickly forgetting her advice about gossip.

Chapter 6

Tina sat on the floor in her bedroom going through her mother's beauty and fashion magazines. She never really paid attention to what the models looked like until now.

She spread the magazines across the bedroom floor so that she could look at each cover. She saw a lot of hair flying everywhere, hands on hips, and plenty of cute clothes. She was puzzled as she read the directions to her homework assignment.

"Ma-ma!" Tina yelled her mother's name until she appeared.

"I'm right here, Scooterbug," her mother said, standing beside her.

Tina passed her worksheet to her mother.

"What does emphasis mean?"

Her mother sat on her bed and read the

I'M CHANGING

directions. "What do you notice about all of the models you see?"

"I think they all look pretty."

"Do you see different body types?"

"Like, none of them are big-boned if that's what you're asking."

"They don't even have to be overweight, but aren't all these models skinny?"

"Yeah."

"What else do you notice if you look at them."

"They look silly poking their shiny lips out. I think they're trying to make them look bigger."

"What else?" her mother asked.

"Oh my goodness," Tina said, looking at the magazines. "Everyone looks kinda perfect."

"Just pay attention to the images that you see. I'm going to let you finish up. Oh no, baby," her mother said, picking up a few of the magazines on Tina's floor. "You can't mess with my Oprah magazines. Looks like I picked up all your magazines with diversity on the cover." Her mother said looking at the magazines on the floor.

When her mother left, Tina looked at the magazines. Now that the Oprah magazines were gone, she didn't see models on the cover with Oprah's skin tone. Maybe she shouldn't be looking at her mother's magazines. She went under Patrice's bed and retrieved some teen magazines. She spread the magazines on the floor and looked at the covers. All of the cover models looked exactly the same.

She skimmed through a few of the magazines, and the more she turned the pages the more questions she had. Why was every girl's hair long? Although Tina had long hair, she thought about girls like Lauren Wright, who didn't. Where was the Asian girl like Marci? Tina's stomach stuck out a little she thought about the girls whose stomachs stuck out a lot. She even thought about girls with bright red hair like Nancy's. She stared at the magazines covers scattered across her floor and realized that diversity wasn't celebrated. She liked her magazines because they had great articles, but now that she was aware that people like her and her friends weren't on the covers and inside the magazines, she was peeved. Tina was happy that she was colorblind, but she wasn't happy that magazines focused on a certain type only. She turned on her computer and emailed Amanda Jo.

I'M CHANGING

Amanda Jo,

I'm so mad!!! Our homework 4 health really got under my skin. Do you know that most magazines only show girls that look like you? What about the girls that don't look like you? What kind of messed up junk is that? Like where are the girls that look like me? Where are my Asian and Latina sisters? Girl these magazines don't represent all of us. All white girls aren't skinny, you know, look at Pepperstank. Well okay she lost a little weight, but she still has that jolly belly. I think we should make up our own magazine. Here are some names for the magazine. Please vote.

- o Babygirl
- o Finally
- o Bona Fide
- o Real

We can write stories and everything. We can have quizzes like, what to do when your BFF's breath stinks? I'm gonna ask Ms. Hogan if we can do this 4 extra credit.

BTW tell your momma that it's okay 2 IM and I-chat. All this typing hurts my fingers.

Chapter 7

When Tina presented the idea of a magazine to Ms. Hogan, she loved it and actually made it a group project for all of the girls. There were plenty of opinions about the name of the magazine.

"Since it was my idea I want to call the magazine *Babygirl* or *Bona Fide*."

"Why Bona Fide?" Nancy asked with her lips twitched up in disgust.

"Bona Fide means real. You know, using a thesaurus could really help you expand your vocabulary."

"Guess she told you," Chante remarked.

"Be quiet, Chante," Nancy and Tina said together.

"I want you ladies to think about the way you speak to one another," Ms. Hogan said. "I hear bossiness and sometimes gossiping."

"Speaking of gossiping," Chante said, crossing her arms, "Ms. Hogan you should've been in third hour yesterday. Louis McDougal was—"

"Gossip, Chante, you're gossiping," Ms. Hogan warned.

"I just thought maybe you'd be interested in knowing that Louis—"

"Quiet!"

"Okay, just don't be surprised when Louis keeps passing gas in your class."

Chante was itching to tell Ms. Hogan about Louis' gas problem, but Ms. Hogan didn't want to hear it. Louis accidentally ate his pregnant aunt's special casserole intended to induce her labor. He passed gas and kept belching throughout the day. Tina tried to think of a new nickname for Louis, but she couldn't come up with anything. She had more important things to think about anyway, like the magazine.

Luck would have it that Nancy's mother volunteered to take some photographs for their student magazine. During one of her visits she came in with her assistant. They showed the class how magazines airbrush photos. She pulled up a photo of a younger Nancy with spaghetti sauce all over her face. The class laughed as they looked at the photo. They were amazed when the assistant clicked on certain parts of Nancy's face and totally erased the spaghetti sauce. They also changed Nancy's eye and hair color. Nancy's mother told the class that this was the same technique that magazines used on models and celebrities to make them look perfect.

Mrs. Pepperdine's assistant showed other examples of Photoshop. They showed a picture of Nancy's grandmother, who had a lot of wrinkles on her face; with a few clicks the wrinkles were gone and Nancy's grandmother looked years younger. They showed a picture of a model, but they made her thighs and arms smaller. The class was amazed by this information. Ms. Hogan thanked Mrs. Pepperdine and her assistant for showing the class about Photoshop techniques. After they left, Ms. Hogan sat on her desk and asked the class how they felt about what they just saw.

"It's not fair," Nancy said. "We're not seeing the truth."

"Exactly," Ms. Hogan said.

"Well, they can airbrush my pictures and take some of my fat away," Lauren said.

"Why would you say something that stupid?" Tina asked.

I'M CHANGING

"It's true, I'm fat and ugly," Lauren said, putting her hands up to her face. "Everybody knows it," she said crying.

"Lauren, you're a beautiful girl," Ms. Hogan reassured her.

"If I was so beautiful then girls like me would be on the cover of magazines. Girls like me would be able to go to the mall and fit a large T-shirt, but they make large T-shirts for small, skinny people! Do you know that I shop at Big Woman's World? That store is for big adult women, women who have careers. I don't dress my age, I dress like a grown working woman. No one makes clothes for girls like me. I just hate that I'm so big, I hate it," Lauren cried.

Chante hugged Lauren. "You know what, Lauren, you are big."

"Shut up," Nancy said.

"Let me finish," Chante said, rubbing Lauren's hair. "So what you're bigger, so what Marci is skinny, Nancy and Ms. Hogan have red hair and freckles, Tina has no sense of style, some people wear glasses, some people are blind, others are in wheelchairs; you have to accept who you are."

"But it's hard," Lauren said, wiping her eyes.

"Some people think I'm nosey and have a big mouth."

"*Some* people?" Tina interrupted. "Everyone knows that you have a big mouth."

"I don't care what people say or what people think about me. People just need to tell me what's going on that way I won't have questions."

Lauren smiled at Chante as the tears rolled down her face. "Thanks, Chante, I hear what you're saying and all, but it's really not that simple. Everywhere I go, everywhere I look, I'm reminded that I'm big."

"It has to be hard for many of you growing up in this image-consumed culture. Mrs. Pepperdine clearly showed us that even models don't look the way we think they look. Chante made some good points; we're all different. Accepting who we are and loving ourselves is the challenge."

"But when you don't see yourself on magazine covers and on television or videos you feel left out," Nancy said, playing with her hair. "Like you don't belong."

"You sure do," Lauren said. She closed her eyes and began to cry again.

Lauren had a lot of hurt and anger inside, and this only made Tina's blood boil. She promised herself that for *Bona Fide's* first edition, Lauren would be their cover model.

I'M CHANGING

Tina took some books out of her book-bag and placed them in her locker. Chante leaned on the locker next to Tina's shaking her head.

"I'm just saying if Lauren is crying all about her weight then maybe, just maybe she needs to lose some."

"It's not just about losing weight Chante," Tina said sorting through her books.

"Then what she crying for?"

"Accepting who you are, being represented in magazines. Feeling left out. You weren't even listening."

"Yes I was. I'm the one who told her to accept who she is. What more can I say? I'm not Tyra Banks. I can't offer her a fashion makeover. I'm just Chante from around the way. Moving on and switching it up— this summer went by real quick didn't it? You and Marci stopped being friends. She started hanging with Nancy. How the heck did that happen? They hated each other now they're dressing alike? Maybe I am Tyra. You wanna tell me what happened?

"Give it up Chante."

"You know I talked to Ms. Hogan about doing some investigative reporting for Bona Fide right?"

Tina ignored Chante. She closed her locker and walked away. Ace stood next to Chante and laughed.

"You're laughing now, but I'm gonna find out what happened. Ba-by, ba-by," Chante said dancing.

Chapter 8

Amanda Jo made the first month of school ease by. Tina couldn't believe how much they had in common. They liked the same singers, TV shows, they even loved the same type of fashions. Besides Amanda Jo's incredibly aggravating laugh, Tina liked everything about her and they became two peas in a pod. They shared their lunches, did word search puzzles together, and made up songs and short stories.

Tina informed Amanda Jo about her rocky history with Nancy and Marci; she even attempted to turn Amanda Jo against them. Instead of being negative, Amanda Jo told her that Marci would realize the mistake she made. She thought that Nancy and Marci were nice, and she didn't want to cause any trouble.

Tina and Marci remained civil to one another, but they certainly kept their distance. There was plenty of eye rolling, sighs when the other gave answers to a question, and slight bumps in the hallway. The only time they really talked was during the health workshop.

Tina thought about the first day of school and how she feared sitting in the cafeteria. She knew wherever she sat, that would eventually be her permanent spot. She had to think carefully about where she wanted to sit and who she wanted to sit by. Tina quickly sat next to Gordon—sitting by a boy was safe. Amanda Jo sat next to her, which was a relief. Tina began to eat her lunch and worried about who would sit across from her. Nancy and Marci looked at the empty space, and with their noses high in the air they decided to sit on the other end of the table. Tina giggled with Amanda Jo, but as soon as she turned to sip her juice box, Chante Baker and Ace Cryer were sitting across from them.

"Boom chaka chaka boom," Ace said, smiling as he put his lunch tray on the table.

"Hey lunch family," Chante coyly said as she sat down. She immediately asked Amanda Jo what she was having for lunch. "You got some okra?"

"Or some pig feet," Ace said, laughing with Chante.

"Not today, but I will bring some in," Amanda Jo joked. "Don't worry, I'll make sure I bring the hot sauce."

"Okay," Ace said, giving Amanda Jo a high-five.

Almost immediately the lunch room was the place to be. There was plenty of comedy and plenty of talking. All the students let loose, but Chante and Ace left Tina's body in pain from laughing so hard. Tina pitied poor little Shadow, who sat at the other end of the table all up in boring Pepperstank's face.

Tina was having the time of her life. Middle school was fun. Besides lunch, walking in the halls was one of her favorite things to do. She loved the crowded halls. She thought it was cool to go to her locker every hour to switch books for the next class, but for some reason she always left something important in her locker. As the weeks went by, Tina received verbal and written notices from her teachers, especially about talking. Her teachers weren't about to ruin her life so the notices never made it home. Why would the teachers even attempt to stop her status as a social butterfly?

Tina's arm was intertwined with Amanda Jo's as they walked to Mr. Baylor's class. Amanda Jo kept running into people because her eyes were glued to a pink worksheet she had in her hand.

"Earth to Amanda Jo," Tina said, trying to get her friend's attention.

"Are you ready for our math test?" Amanda Jo asked.

"What math test?"

"The test we're about to take on the order of operations," she said, holding her up pink worksheet.

"That's today?"

"How could you forget? Mr. Baylor made us put it in our student planner."

"I keep forgetting; my planner is at home somewhere." Tina laughed. "I have to buy a new one at the student store. Please remind me."

"Are you at least prepared for the test? I mean, I know you've been busier than ants at a Sunday picnic, but we got a test, girl."

"I have been busy; cleaning up, on the computer, taking Jerry out to use it—I just got a lot going on. Let me see the review sheet again," Tina said, glaring at the pink paper. "Oh yeah, I got this test on lock, piece of cake, I can take this test with my eyes closed."

I'M CHANGING

Tina peeled the fingernail polish off her nails. She tapped her pencil on the desk. She bit her bottom lip. She was nervous, very nervous as she looked at the math test on her desk. *The order of operations, why does this look so different?* Tina thought. There was no way she could solve the problems without knowing the formula. She took her finger and began to twist her hair. P is for parenthesis, E is for exponents…she guessed the rest. *What was that phrase Mr. Baylor taught us to help solve the order of operations? Please Excuse My Dear Aunt Sally—that's it!* Tina wrote down the formula and began to work on the first problem. She hesitated, then paused. *That's not it; it's Please My Dear Aunt Eleanor Stay—that's it.* Tina erased the old formula and wrote the new one. She struggled throughout the test. When class was over she felt numb.

"Oh my goodness, that test was hard," Amanda Jo said. "I was nervous as a cow with a bucktooth calf."

"So was I, but I wouldn't exactly use that phrase," Tina said. She didn't understand why math was difficult for her now. She always got

A's in math back at Kellwagen. She took a deep breath, then started gossiping about LaKiesha Robinson.

The next day Mr. Baylor passed out the test results from the math quiz putting them face down on each student's desk. Tina could feel her stomach growling. Chante slowly lifted her paper to see her grade. She smiled, then whispered her grade to Ace. Tina read her lips. *If Chante got an A, I know I must have a B.* The bell rang and Mr. Baylor dismissed the class. Amanda Jo and Tina didn't look at their results until they were in the hallway.

"Well, butter my butt and call me a biscuit, I got an A on my quiz." Amanda Jo danced.

"I hope you know that you're country," Tina said, looking at her paper.

"More country than cornflakes, that's what my Auntie Kitty Lee says. What you get on your quiz?"

"Not an A," Tina said in a disappointed whisper.

"What you get then, a B…?"

Tina was quiet.

"C…D…F?" Amanda Jo guessed.

There was a long pause.

"You got an F, dawgonnit," Amanda Jo said.

"You can say that again," Tina said, leaning against her locker.

"How do you feel?"

"It's hard to explain. I feel confused, stupid."

"Dumber than a stump?"

"I guess," Tina somberly said.

"Bless your heart," Amanda Jo said, hugging her friend.

Adjusting to middle school in terms of doing the work was proving to be a bit challenging for Tina. Keeping up with the different classes and turning in assignments made her head spin. All the teachers wanted something; a project, a parent's signature, completed assignments; it was too much. Although she was having fun socializing, studying and getting good grades was the hard part.

Later that day in Literature Tina was supposed to be reading, but instead she passed Amanda Jo a note inviting her over for the weekend. Amanda Jo was so happy she immediately said she'd come over.

Five minutes before the bell rang, Mrs. Simmons announced that cheerleading tryouts would begin at the end of the month. The girls in the class clapped and cheered in excitement. Tina could feel her stomach twisting in knots. Last year she didn't make the fifth grade cheer team because Nancy took the last spot. It didn't help that Tina didn't know how to do a cartwheel. Nancy didn't hesitate to rub it in. To make matters worse, Nancy, along with the rest of the squad, got their picture in the local newspaper.

On the bus ride home, thoughts of making the cheer team danced in Tina's head. Her stomach began to ache. She took a deep breath, and then closed her eyes. Determined to make the squad, Tina declared to herself that she would practice every day after school and she did.

Chapter 9

The verdict was in Tina hated the combined health class. She often drifted off and thought about the old days back at Kellwagen Elementary. Tina didn't understand the purpose for having the combined health class it was stupid. Because she was bored she wrote notes to Amanda Jo.

Ms. Hogan allowed students to sit wherever they wanted, and for Tina that meant sitting at the back table with Amanda Jo, Louis, Chante, and Ace. They would laugh, joke, and sneak candy. Ms. Hogan constantly had to tell their table to be quiet.

"What should I bring to wear when I come over to your house?" Amanda Jo whispered.

"Just bring something to sleep in and something to wear on Saturday," Tina said.

"What should I bring?" Louis joked.

"Some thongs," Ace said.

The table giggled.

"Good afternoon, class," Ms. Hogan said, standing in front of her desk. "Today we'll be discussing something that is quite personal, but very necessary."

Ms. Hogan walked to the green chalkboard and wrote the word "HYGIENE" on the board. The class began to laugh.

"Pay attention, Daniel," Ace said loudly.

"Be quiet before you get hurt," Daniel threatened.

"You hurt me every day with that breath," Ace said.

The class continued to laugh.

"One more crack and you'll both be in detention," Ms. Hogan warned.

"Crack—that's somewhere Daniel doesn't wash," Chante whispered.

Tina and Amanda Jo held in their laughter, but Ace couldn't. Everyone in the class turned to their table. Tina and Amanda Jo smiled, putting their hands over their mouths. Marci and Tina's eyes met; they quickly turned their heads when they realized they were looking at each other.

"Quiet back there," Ms. Hogan said. "It is very important to keep your body clean. Let's

I'M CHANGING

face it, you're growing up and your body is going through changes. Now, last week in our workshops we discussed puberty. We talked about all of the physical changes your body is going through. Can someone raise their hand and tell me some of the things that happen during puberty?"

Many students raised their hands. Tina doodled hearts on her notebook for the boy she loved since the third grade, Christopher Edwards.

"You begin to have these feelings for the opposite sex," Nancy said.

"Or the same sex," Louis joked, looking at Ace.

"Don't go there, Louis," Ace said.

"Correct, Nancy," Ms. Hogan said, ignoring Louis and Ace. "Yes, Chante?"

Tina looked up and couldn't believe that Chante was participating.

"You grow hair under your arms and on your private area," she said, smiling.

Ms. Hogan wrote pubic hair on the board. Tina continued to trace the heart she made over and over. *I love me some Christopher.*

"Don't forget hair grows on the legs, face, and chest," Ms. Hogan added.

"Girls grow hair on their chest?" Lauren innocently asked.

"Nancy does," Joseph Alexander teased.

"I need some maturity, children," Ms. Hogan said. "And speaking of maturity, it is also known that during puberty girls experience their growth spurt a lot sooner than boys, which is why some of you girls are taller than boys." The girls taunted the boys.

"But," Ms. Hogan said, "Boys will have a rapid growth spurt later in adolescence and in many cases they will become a lot taller than you girls."

The boys had their turn to taunt.

Tina continued to make heart doodles in her notebook. She felt that Ms. Hogan's combined class was a waste of time. She read all of the things Ms. Hogan wrote on the board: attraction for boys/girls, weight gain, menstrual cycle, acne, voice deepens, height increases, and hair growth. She decided to write a note to Amanda Jo.

> This is so boring. Duh, of course we grow up, it's called being a teenager. I wonder if Christopher has hair on his chest. I forgot to tell you to bring something to cheer in. We're going to practice in the family room and we're gonna work on the magazine too. We're gonna have so much fun!!!!!!!

Tina passed the note to Amanda Jo. Ms. Hogan wiped her hands of excess chalk. She leaned against her desk and crossed her arms.

"Keeping your body clean is very important. I know that you're in middle school, but many parents assume that you know how to wash your body properly. Unfortunately many of you do not wash behind your ears, you totally neglect your necks, and oh brother, let's talk about those teeth, under those arms, and in those private areas. There's nothing worse than having people talk about the way you smell."

"Preach, Ms. Hogan," Chante said, clapping her hands together.

"Let's start by talking about soap and water," Ms. Hogan said.

"Speak up, Ms. Hogan, some people in here need to hear you," Ace dramatically said. "Shhh, y'all need to be quiet and listen seriously!"

"Soap, water, toothpaste, cotton swabs, lotion, powder, dental floss, mouthwash, and clean clothes are your friends," Ms. Hogan said.

The class laughed, but they were deeply captivated by the words their teacher had to say.

"Speak, speak," Chante said as if she were at a Baptist church Sunday service.

"Sometimes, some people like to diss their friends," Ms. Hogan said.

"Oh my God, Ms. Hogan said dissed," Ace said, laughing.

"Let's cool it with the outbursts. When you diss your friends, you don't smell good, your ears are waxy, your skin is dry, you have tarter buildup, your breath stinks, and your clothes are dirty. Not a good look or smell by any means. The bottom line is you don't want to diss your friends. You need to have a wonderful relationship with your friends. Let me give you some pointers on how to stay clean. I know that you all are young adults, but there's nothing wrong with having a review on hygiene."

The class laughed. Some students pointed fingers at other students while Ms. Hogan was facing the board.

After listening to Ms. Hogan to some extent lecture for thirty minutes, Tina was so happy when the bell rang. As she walked down the hall, she couldn't believe her eyes. Christopher Edwards, the boy she'd adored since the third grade, gave Marci a hug then went to his locker. Tina didn't know what to do; she wanted to cry, but she was too full of anger toward Marci. She knew that Tina loved Christopher Edwards. Marci knew that Tina made up fake names

I'M CHANGING

for their future kids Christina and CJ. It was time that Tina gave Marci a piece of her mind.

Marci was putting her books in her locker when Tina approached her.

"You think you're slick," Tina said.

Marci turned facing Tina. "What are you talking about?"

"Hugging Christopher, that's what."

"Newsflash, Tina, he doesn't like you."

"Says who? Did he tell you he doesn't like me?"

"I asked him if he thought you were cute, and he said you're okay," Marci said, closing her locker.

"I don't believe you."

"Well, believe this, Christopher and I go together. Get over it, *little girl*," Marci said, pointing her finger in Tina's face.

"I'm older than you," Tina said, moving Marci's finger.

"But you act younger than me. Still playing dolls in the sixth grade."

"I like my dolls and I don't care what you think. You need to start being yourself instead of trying to be like Pepperstank. I liked you a lot better then, Shadow," Tina said, walking away.

"Would you just chill out for a minute? I was going to tell you that I really don't—" Marci was too frustrated with Tina to say anything.

"What? What do you have to say to me?" Tina said putting her hands on her hips. Marci didn't say anything. Tina rolled her eyes. By the time she walked over to her locker Christopher gave Marci another hug. Marci looked at Tina.

"Don't stare," Amanda Jo said, standing beside her. "Anyway, I'm going to come over right after school tomorrow."

"Okay," Tina said.

"See you tomorrow," Amanda Jo said with her irritating laugh.

Tina opened her locker and grabbed her jacket. Tina peeked over to Marci's locker. She was alone now. She stared at Tina with a sad look on her face. Tina stared back at her former best friend. Tina couldn't believe how much Marci changed. All she ever talked about to Marci was her crush on Christopher Edwards and now she's dating him.

"I think we should talk Tina," Marci said across the hall.

"We don't have anything, nothing, nada to talk about," Tina said as she slammed her locker.

Chapter 10

Tina dropped her book bag on the kitchen floor. Jerry greeted her with his usual barking. Her mother was sitting at the kitchen table drinking juice and reading a magazine with a baby on it.

"What are you reading, Mom?"

Her mother looked at the cover of the magazine. "A fertility magazine honey."

Tina didn't know what fertility meant and she certainly didn't want to know.

"How was school?"

She gave her mother a kiss, then opened the refrigerator. "Fine."

"What did you learn?"

"We did a review of cell structures in science, puberty in health. Mom, can you go grocery shopping?"

"I'm going on Saturday. What are you looking for?"

"Something good," Tina sulked. "All of this food is boring. Amanda Jo isn't going to eat any of this."

"Amanda Jo?"

"Yeah, she's sleeping over tomorrow."

"Says who?"

"Mom, I know you are not bugging out about Amanda Jo coming over."

"You didn't ask me," her mother said. "Did you ask your father?"

"No," Tina said nonchalantly.

"So you're just doing what you want to do?"

"Mom, I already invited Amanda Jo and she said she's coming," Tina whined.

"Well, you're just going to have to tell her she can't come."

"Why not?" she said, making her voice louder.

"Because I said so, young lady."

"But Patrice is allowed to have company."

"I know Patrice's friends."

"Amanda Jo is a good person," Tina pleaded.

"That's not the point."

"You never want me to have fun!"

I'M CHANGING

"I don't know this Amanda Jo girl or her parents."

"I talk about her all the time. She's my best friend."

"Since when? Marci is your best friend."

"If you were paying attention you would know that Marci doesn't come over anymore."

"You better lower your voice, Scooterbug. I do pay attention and I have noticed Marci's absence. What happened?"

"Can Amanda Jo come over?"

"What happened with Marci?"

"Can Amanda Jo come over?"

"I don't like the way you're addressing me. Amanda Jo can't come over, so call her and tell her another time."

"But, Mom," Tina sobbed.

"I said no," her mother said, walking out the kitchen.

Tina slammed the refrigerator door and said when the coast was clear, "You make me sick."

Her mother walked back in the kitchen.

"I'm about to make you sicker. You're grounded, now go to your room," her mother demanded.

Tina screamed, then ran up the stairs.

Patrice was sitting on the bed watching videos when Tina barged into the room crying. Patrice was two years older than Tina. She was very sophisticated for her age. Her clothes were neatly pressed, and her hair never had a strand out of place. Everything had to be neat for Patrice. Her side of the closet was color-coded and organized. Tina was the complete opposite; she was messy. Her side of the room had clothes and unfinished art projects on the floor. Tina walked over to the television and turned it off.

"What is your problem?" her sister asked.

"You're my problem. Why don't you move or something?"

Patrice stood up and put her hands on her hips.

"Yeah, I'm feeling a little froggy," Tina said.

"Well, take a leap."

Tina pushed her sister, making her fall on the bed. The sisters fought. They kicked, hit, and threw objects at each other. They knocked over books and pulled the comforters off their beds as they rumbled on them.

I'M CHANGING

"What is going on in here?" their mother said, walking in the room. "Stop it." Patrice gave Tina a final hit on the arm.

"Ouch," Tina yelled, rubbing her arm.

"Tina came in here with a major attitude, turned off the television, and then pushed me," Patrice said, listing Tina's offenses on her fingers.

"Scooterbug, clean up this mess," her mother said.

"But Patrice made it too."

"You've been in a bad mood ever since you got home."

"It's not fair."

"Since when have you been so defiant? You're talking back, making plans without asking, picking fights with your sister. Not to mention you're talking to me like I'm one of your little friends. I'm very disappointed in your behavior, and your father will be too."

"Don't tell him, Mom. I'm really sorry," Tina cried.

"Oh so you don't care if I'm disappointed in your behavior. Girl clean this mess up. Patrice, go watch videos down in the den," her mother said.

Patrice walked out of the room, then stuck her tongue out at Tina.

"I didn't do all of this by myself," Tina pouted.

"Did you call Amanda Jo yet?"

"I'm about to. Mom, Patrice made this mess too!"

"While you're cleaning I want you to think about your behavior."

"Why are you treating me like Cinderella?"

"Zip those lips right now. I don't want to hear anything else out of your mouth," her mother said, closing the door.

Tina looked around her messy room. She picked up her pillow from the floor and began to squeeze it. She pretended that the pillow was Patrice, Marci, and her mother; everyone was making her mad.

Tina didn't come out of her room for the rest of the day. She didn't even eat dinner. She watched television and read a book. Later in the evening she heard her father's car pull up in the driveway. She quickly ran to her bed and closed her eyes pretending she was asleep. About ten minutes later Tina could hear her mother informing her father of the day's events.

"I don't know what's wrong with your foolish child," her mother said.

I'M CHANGING

Tina opened her mouth in surprise. She couldn't believe her mother called her foolish and referred to her as being his child only.

"What did Patrice do?" her father asked.

"No, it's Scooterbug. She talked back to me and even said I made her sick."

"Sure does," Tina murmured.

"Where is she?" her father asked.

"In her room," her mother said.

"Seems like she needs a little heart to heart with dear old dad."

"Honey, I packed your bags for your trip."

Tina forgot that her dad was flying out of town for a few days. She hated when her father had to leave—he was the nice one.

"I'm just going to run up for a second," her father said.

Tina closed her eyes. She could hear her father's footsteps coming toward her room. He turned the doorknob and whispered her name. Tina could feel her father's eyes on her, but she remained still as a rock. Would he believe that she fell asleep at 7:30 p.m.? He kissed her on the forehead then closed the door. Tina opened her eyes and exhaled in relief.

The next morning Tina awakened to weird stomach pains. She rubbed her stomach and looked over to Patrice's adjacent canopy bed. Patrice was sleeping like a bear. How much Patrice irked her. She got away with not cleaning the room. If her stomach didn't hurt she'd jump on top of Patrice and give her a wakeup call all right. She stared at her sister sleeping with her eye mask on and shook her head in disgust. Tina thought about what she had to do today. She had to tell Amanda Jo that she couldn't come over. *It's so unfair*, Tina thought. She closed her eyes and went back to sleep.

Chapter 11

"Wake up, divas," their mother said.

Patrice quickly got up and began to make her bed while Tina stayed in hers.

"Ouch," Tina moaned as her stomach cramped.

"I hope you're in a better mood today," her mother said, kissing her.

"My stomach hurts," she complained. "I don't feel good."

"She's just trying to stay home so that she doesn't have to face her little friend who can't sleep over," Patrice said.

"Trust me, Patrice, I'm on to Scooterbug," her mother said.

"I'm serious, my stomach does hurt."

"You know, Tina," Patrice said. "You're like a clear glass vase. We can see right through you."

"Scooterbug, get out of bed," her mother demanded.

Tina snatched her covers off and stomped to the bathroom. Her stomach really did hurt, but it didn't matter; they didn't believe her anyway. She pulled her hair back in one ball. She began to think of Christopher Edwards as she stared at her reflection in the mirror. Since Christopher liked girls who wore lip gloss and carried purses, maybe she should spice up her appearance. When Patrice went downstairs for breakfast, Tina quickly went into the closet and took Patrice's black leather designer purse. She walked over to the vanity and took one of Patrice's sparkling lip glosses. She stuffed the items in her book bag. She felt like she was missing something that's when she noticed her dolls makeup kit on the floor. She took the eye shadow compact and smiled. Tina looked at her reflection in the mirror and blew herself a kiss.

A glossy-lipped Tina closed her locker door only to be greeted by Amanda Jo.

"Good morning," Amanda Jo said, smiling.

I'M CHANGING

Tina was startled. How would she tell her new best friend that she couldn't spend the night? She couldn't bring herself to call Amanda Jo last night. She thought it would be better telling her face to face. "Hey," she said softly.

"Oh my goodness, you're wearing lip gloss. And what's that gold or yellow eye shadow? It sure does look purty on you."

"Thanks."

"All of my stuff can't fit in my locker, so Mrs. Simmons is going to keep my bag in her closet."

How was she going to tell Amanda Jo that she couldn't come over?

"We're going to have so much fun. I snuck my brother's MP3. There are songs on there that are so filthy, when we get finished listening to them, girl, we're gonna have to clean our ears with buckets of soapy water. Ha-ha-he-he-haw-he," Amanda Jo laughed.

Tina's mouth dropped. "Wow, profanity. My mother only lets me listen to the radio versions of songs."

Tina wanted to cry how much she wanted to hang out with Amanda Jo; if only her mother was from the planet Earth. It was as if Patrice and her mother were plotting against her to make her life miserable. She could hear her mother's voice telling her that Amanda Jo couldn't come over. *No more playing games,* Tina said to herself taking a deep breath, "About tonight."

Amanda Jo jumped up and down in excitement. "I am so happy you invited me over, Tina. My first sleepover in Michigan, oh boy! Ever since I moved here I've been by my lonesome until I met you. I know I got my big brother, Ashton Leigh, he's eighteen, and then there's my little sister, Cassidy Reign, but she's only three months bless her little whittle, whittle cute heart, I just needed a friend. You are my true friend Tina. Enough of that though, so I got Curtis to give me Christopher Edwards phone number so you can call him tonight," Amanda Jo snorkeled in her infamous laugh.

The bell rang. Everyone quickly ran to their classes. Tina felt horrible. How was she going to break the news to Amanda Jo? Fourth period was almost over and Tina still hadn't told Amanda Jo that she couldn't spend the night. Mr. Werner asked Nancy to pass out the weekend homework worksheets. The class began to chatter when Mr. Werner searched through his desk. Tina finally decided to tell Amanda Jo the truth. Amanda Jo sat

I'M CHANGING

directly in front of Tina. She paused several times before tapping her shoulder, but finally she did.

"Hey, girl," Amanda Jo said, smiling.

It was as if a light was shining on her. She looked so happy. *Are her eyes twinkling?* Tina asked herself. *Oh brother, this is going to be hard.*

"What's wrong? You look like you just lost the remote to the TV."

"I have some really bad news. I don't know how to tell you, but—"

Amanda Jo made her eyes big. "What is it? Spit it out before you choke."

Tina bit her bottom lip. Her voice was shaky. "My mother said that you can't come over."

Nancy was standing in front of Amanda Jo's desk when Tina made her announcement. "Here are your worksheets," Nancy said, quickly giving Amanda Jo enough worksheets for her row.

"What do you mean?" Amanda Jo asked somberly.

"My mother said that I didn't ask her in advance."

"Well, why didn't you call me?" Amanda Jo said loudly.

"I tried to, but your line was busy," Tina lied. "I'm sorry. I really do want you to come over."

"Pass back the worksheets," Daniel Tucker yelled.

Amanda Jo took a worksheet and threw the rest on Tina's desk. "Tina, don't you sit in front of my face and tell me a lie. I've known you for almost two months and I know when you're fibbing a big one. How could you? I never thought you'd be faker than instant mashed potatoes."

"I'm not, I'm real," Tina pleaded. "I'm better than instant mashed potatoes. I'm like cheesy scalloped potatoes with bacon bits!"

"Fake bacon bits that is!" Amanda Jo frowned.

"The worksheets, ladies," Daniel yelled. In a rage Tina got up from her desk with the remaining worksheets. She smacked them on top of Daniel's desk and gave him the meanest look. "HERE!"

"Dang, Boo Boo, is it that time of the month?" Ace said, reaching his hand out to give Chante the traditional high-five.

Chapter 12

Tina couldn't believe how Amanda Jo ignored her for the remainder of the day. The last time she felt this bad was when Marci bailed out on her. She felt awful, and the jokes from Ace and Chante weren't helping or the stares from Nancy and Marci.

It was last period and Mrs. Simmons read a passage from the latest classroom story, Helen Keller. Ace and Louis seemed to be the only students paying attention. Maybe Mrs. Simmons didn't get the memo Tina thought, they read Helen Keller back at Kellwagen.

"Okay, class," Mrs. Simmons said, closing her book. "In the opening scene, Helen is very ill. What illness does she have?"

Mrs. Simmons looked directly at Tina. Ace raised his hand, shaking it like he had a seizure in his arm.

"Tina Morten?"

"Umm, Helen was sleepy?" Tina said with uncertainty.

Mrs. Simmons called on Louis.

"Helen had a fever that left her blind and deaf," Louis answered. "I do believe the doctor said she had acute congestion of the brain and stomach. Correct me if I'm wrong, Mrs. Simmons." Louis was one of the class clowns, but he was very smart. He never hesitated to show off those smarts.

"Very, very good, Louis," Mrs. Simmons said.

Whatever, Tina thought. At least she tried. Tina rolled her eyes and made a face at Louis.

"How does Kate Keller discover that Helen is blind and deaf?" Mrs. Simmons asked.

Tina opened Patrice's black leather purse. She raked through the items inside. Patrice had; ten dollars, a brush, some gum, the tube of cherry-flavored lip gloss that she stole, her dolls eye shadow, and folded pieces of paper. Tina put some of the lip gloss on her lips; then she opened one of the notes. It was a permission slip to The Science Center.

"This is why you aren't paying attention," Mrs. Simmons said, taking the note and the purse.

"But, it isn't mine, it's my—"

I'M CHANGING

Mrs. Simmons interrupted. "Go to my desk and put the purse in my top drawer." The class laughed as Tina slowly walked to Mrs. Simmons' desk.

Who does Mrs. Simmons think she is? She is not my mother. Why is she trying to embarrass me? Tina placed the purse in the drawer. On her way back to her desk, Tina noticed Chante passing a note to Amanda Jo. Amanda Jo quickly took the letter and read it. What was Chante giving Amanda Jo a note for? Amanda Jo balled up the paper. Tina stared at the balled-up note on the edge of her desk and wondered about its content. Was it about her?

Mrs. Simmons continued the Helen Keller discussion. Tina looked at the clock on the wall; she was ready to go home, and she wanted to go to sleep. She yawned, then stared at the green chalkboard. She remembered the days when she washed the board for Mr. Greenberg back at Kellwagen. She loved being the board captain. She wondered what Mr. Greenberg was doing right now. Being in class all day was mind-numbing for Tina. *Shoot, we should have recess,* she told herself. *They expect us to pay attention to this boring crap all day without going outside to play, this is so lame. I'm so hungry. I have the taste for a bacon cheeseburger with crispy French fries that sounds so dang on good.* Tina bit her bottom lip and took a hard swallow; then she took a long yawn. *Wake up, girl, wake up,* she thought, making her eyes big. She wiped her eyes, then tapped her pencil on her desk.

"Class, put your things away," Mrs. Simmons said.

Thank goodness, Tina said to herself, looking at the clock. She yawned again and began to straighten up her work area.

"Progress reports," Mrs. Simmons said, taking a manila folder out of her desk drawer.

Tina dropped her pencil on the floor. It felt like she was having a panic attack. She totally forgot about progress reports. *Well, maybe it's not as bad as I think.* Mrs. Simmons passed the yellow progress reports out alphabetically. She called the names quickly.

"How do you think you did?" Tina said to Amanda Jo.

"Amanda Jo Fields," Mrs. Simmons said, giving Amanda Jo her progress report. Amanda Jo read her markings.

"What did you get?"

"Grades," Amanda Jo snapped.

"Yeah baby, yeah baby, yeah baby," Joseph Alexander said, dancing as he read his progress report. "I'm getting off my punishment."

I'M CHANGING

"Finally. You've been on that punishment since fifth grade," Chante said.

"I get to play video games, I get to get on the computer and go to my favorite website, www dot nakedness dot com, baby," Joseph said.

The class laughed. Mrs. Simmons didn't hear Joseph. *How convenient*, Tina said to herself. Mrs. Simmons called Marci's name. Marci immediately began to cry. Tina knew that Marci must have gotten some bad markings. She was an overachiever, and anything less than an A was unacceptable. *She deserves to get a bad grade*, Tina thought. *Maybe she'll turn back into the old Marci.*

"I guess hanging around Nancy isn't so glamorous," Tina said to Amanda Jo, who didn't respond.

The bell rang. "If you have your report then you're dismissed," Mrs. Simmons said passing out more reports. "Louis McDougal, Tina Morten…"

Tina eyes quickly scanned the progress report. She froze when she saw her grades, especially her math and health grades. She was in a living nightmare. This had to be one of the lowest points of her life. Her shocked but defeated eyes were glued to the red F. She had never received anything lower than a B ever. She took short breaths. She walked to her desk to gather her books, and tears filled her eyes. As Tina picked up her books, she noticed the balled-up note on the floor beside Amanda Jo's desk. She placed her books back on her desk and opened the paper.

> Since when does she ware lip gloss and eye shadow? What did she do to you? Why do you look like you want to cry? You shoud tell me. Let me give you some backgroun on your girl. She is not a real frend because freens don't make you cry. If I was you I wood stop hanging with her because she ain't real. You know that's why Marcy not her fiend. She is facke. We read Helen Keller in ellamentry. How she get that easy answer wrong? We will talk online 2nite. Hold up do you have IM yet??? Cuz I herd you didn't.
> Chante
> Aka
> Hot Mamma

Leave it up to Chante to write a poorly written note. Despite being talked about, Tina picked up her books and headed for her locker. Amanda Jo was standing waiting for her.

"How did you do?" Amanda Jo said. Tina didn't say anything. "So what are you going to do this weekend?"

"Now you're talking to me?"

"Imagine if your best friend hung you out to dry,"

"But I didn't, I wanted you to come over. I can't help it if my momma is evil. I even told her that she makes me sick and once I said that she grounded me."

"Sure you did," Amanda Jo said. "When do you get off your punishment?"

"I-don't-know," Tina said, raising her voice.

"You don't have to have a funky attitude with me."

"You're the one who has the funky attitude," Tina said, opening her locker.

"When you get off your punishment let me know," Amanda Jo said, walking away.

"Don't forget to work on your cheers for tryouts next week," Tina said, putting her books away.

"Oh I will," Amanda Jo sneered. "Trust me, I will. Have a good weekend."

"I'm grounded. How is my weekend going to be good?" Tina said, slamming her locker.

Chapter 13

Tina sat in the living room on the sofa. She flipped through the pages of one of her teen magazines. Her mother sat beside her and pulled the magazine out of her hand.

"Mom, why did you do that? I'm doing research for *Bona Fide*."

"Your teacher called. She told me that she took your purse. I know that it wasn't your purse because you don't have a purse—it was your sister's," Tina's mother scolded. "Her permission slip was in her purse. She missed the field trip because of you. What is going on with you?"

Tina let out a sigh. "I don't know."

"Go to your room right now," her mother demanded.

Tina reluctantly stood before her mom. She knew it wasn't a good idea to tell her mother about

I'M CHANGING

her progress report, but shouldn't she be honest? Should she tell her mother the truth? Her mother couldn't handle the truth, not all in one day. *When the time is right I'll tell her.*

Tina was afraid to walk in her room. She was certain that Patrice was going to kill her for stealing her purse. When Tina opened her bedroom door, Patrice was watching videos while talking on her cell phone and didn't notice Tina walking in. She took baby steps as she walked over to the closet. She took her progress report out of her book bag and looked at the red F in sorrow. She folded the paper and put it in her back pocket.

"Well, I'll be ready around six…see you then, bye," Patrice said, ending her call. Patrice stared at Tina, then shook her head in disappointment. "Well, well, well, if it isn't Miss I *love* being in trouble. Miss I *love* to talk back to Mom, Miss I *love* to invite company over without permission, steal from my sister, and have temper tantrums all day."

"Be quiet," Tina said, flopping on her bed.

"You know, Tina, lately you have been acting like a real pain in the butt. I mean you are a pain in the butt, always have been, but lately it's like you're…" Patrice switched thoughts. "Have you ever tried to eat outside and a fly just tries to hawk your food? It's buzzing and circling around you, and you're trying to hit it, but it just won't go away? Well, Tina, you're like that fly—irritating."

"Eat liver. Anyway, where are you going?"

"To the movies with LaToya."

"Why do you get to go somewhere?"

Patrice fixed her hair in the mirror, then pointed her index finger in Tina's face.

"I shouldn't even be talking to you. You got my purse taken that contained some crucial items. Luckily for you, sweetheart, I didn't want to go on that stupid field trip, but you better get my purse back from that teacher of yours."

"Get your finger out of my face," Tina said, hitting her sister's hand.

"If I hit you back we'll fight, and you'll get in trouble." Patrice laughed. "But what does it matter, you're already in trouble." Patrice hit Tina. Tina wanted to retaliate, but she stood still. Patrice smiled, then opened the bedroom door.

"You better run," Tina said, sitting on the bed.

"Oh, are you threatening me?" Patrice said, standing in the doorway. "Hey, Mom, Tina is picking a fight with me."

"Mom," Patrice yelled, standing in the hallway.

Tina tried to put her hands over Patrice's mouth, but her sister pushed her away. Patrice purposely repeated their mother's name until she came out of her bedroom. Jerry ran out the room with her, barking. "What is going on? You guys know that I'm trying to rest."

"Your little monster is picking another fight with me."

"Am not."

"Oh, so you are a little monster?" Patrice teased.

"You better stop telling stories," Tina whined.

"She's just mad because I'm going to the movies."

"I don't care about you going to the movies."

"I want you two separated. Patrice go downstairs and wait for LaToya. Tina, you go to your room."

"Can I get my brown purse out of the room, not the black one that Tina stole, but my brown purse?" Patrice asked.

"Hurry up," her mother said.

Jerry nestled in the hallway corner. Patrice quickly came out of the room with the purse. She gave her mother a white sheet of paper.

"What's this?" her mother said, yawning again.

"My progress report," Patrice boastfully said. "Where's yours, Tina? In your back pocket perhaps?" she said, winking at Tina.

"Look at this progress report!" Tina's mom said, pacing the floor.

"Shame, shame, shame," Patrice said, shaking her head.

"What happened to all the A's you used to get?"

"Notice how you said 'used to,' Mom?" Patrice said in a low whisper.

"Let's go to your room, Scooterbug."

"Yeah, come on, let's go," Patrice said, walking toward their bedroom.

"I'm not talking to you. I need to talk to your sister."

"No offense, Mom, but Tina is beyond being talked to. What she needs is a good old-fashioned Alabama-style butt whooping."

Tina remembered what an Alabama-style butt whooping was. According to Patrice people from

I'M CHANGING

Alabama didn't believe in spanking their children they believed in *whooping* their kids with belts, and extension cords. Since both her parents were born in Alabama Tina made sure she was always on her best behavior.

"Downstairs now Patrice!"

Her mother gestured for Tina to lead the way to the bedroom. "You didn't make your bed this morning," she said as she walked into the room.

"Mom, I hate making my bed. It doesn't make sense to make the bed when all I'm going to do is mess it up, and it's not like I'm allowed to have company up here."

"Watch it. Why is Patrice's side of the closet clean and yours isn't?"

"Because this closet just isn't big enough for the both of us."

"Look at this," her mother said, looking at the tall pile of clothes on the closet floor. She picked up a handful of dirty clothes. "Scooterbug, your side of the closet is a mess; this is just pitiful." She held up a pair of blue jeans with a white Popsicle wrapper with dried-up orange syrup attached.

"I meant to throw that away."

"You need to get organized. Do you know what I found under the sofa in the family room?"

"Please tell me that you found my other white gym shoe, with the red hearts on the side. I have been looking all over for that shoe."

"You can't be serious, silly girl. I found your student planner."

"My who?"

"You heard me, your student planner, the one you're supposed to fill out every day."

"Who told you that?"

"Your teacher."

"Which one?"

"Stop it."

"Stop what?"

"Apparently you don't remember that Mrs. Simmons talked about student planners during Open House. I don't understand why you're being very irresponsible."

"Mom, I'm doing the best I can."

"No you're not—look at you, look at your hair and your clothes. You act as if you don't care."

"You bought me this outfit, remember?" Tina softly said.

"I remember how nice it looked this morning. Most of your lunch is on your clothes. I see mustard and chocolate stains," her mother said, looking at Tina's blouse. "If you're not organized

I'M CHANGING

at home and with your appearance, then how are you supposed to be organized in school?"

"That's a really good question," Tina said, crossing her arms.

"Your progress report is bad because you don't have any organizational skills."

"I'm trying."

"No you aren't. How can you go from all A's at Kellwagen to the progress report you have now?"

"Because Kellwagen's work was way easier."

"All I hear is excuses."

"But it's true," Tina said, with tears filling her eyes. "Middle school is different. It's like you have to go to your lockers, write in your planner and have your parents sign it every day, and then—"

Her mother interrupted. "Hold up, sign your planner? I don't remember hearing anything about signing your planner. I know I never signed your planner."

Tina bit her bottom lip.

"It's funny because when I asked your dad about your planner, he said he had never seen it, so if he never saw it, he never signed it."

Tina's eyes shuffled with nervousness. She silently said to herself, *Oh please, oh please, don't ask Mom.*

"So that leaves me with one big question, Tina Kaley Morten. Who signed your planner?"

Silence filled the room. Tina didn't know what to do. Should she fess up? Was her mother going to give her one of those Alabama butt whoopings?

"Scooterbug, you're changing."

"I'm changing?"

"Yes, you are," her mother said. "I'm going to your school to talk to your teacher."

"But, Mom, it's too late—it's Friday," Tina said with relief. "The teachers have gone home by now."

"Not Mrs. Simmons. She told me she's staying late today. Remember, I talked to her earlier about the purse, and she told me that I could stop by and pick it up before 4:30, and it's 2:50 right now," her mother said, looking at her watch. "I just have to check with the main office first."

Tina prayed that the main office would be closed. Just her luck, her principal, Dr. Rouse, arranged for her mother to visit Mrs. Simmons. Tina's stomach growled in fear.

"Mom, you really don't need to talk to Mrs. Simmons. I mean, she spoke her peace on my progress report. Why go up there? You know you could email her about any concerns you may have.

I'M CHANGING

Why waste your gas? I personally think Linton Hall is kinda crazy. Who gives out progress reports on Friday's? Patrice had a field trip on a Friday. They're kinda dumb, don't you think? Mom, don't do this. I know what I need to do. Please, Mom, don't do this, please," Tina pleaded.

"Too late," her mother said. "You're hiding something and I'm about to find out what it is."

Chapter 14

"Please have a seat," Mrs. Simmons said.

Mrs. Morten sat in a wooden chair across from Mrs. Simmons' desk. She set Tina's book bag beside her on the floor.

"It's nice to see you again."

"You too. The last time we saw each other was at the mall. Tina thinks that you saw her butt naked."

Mrs. Simmons laughed. "Tina is something else."

"Yes, she is," her mother agreed.

"I guess I would feel the same way, but please assure her that I only saw her face."

"I'll do that. Thanks for making this exception to see me so late."

"I stay late on Fridays so that I can complete my lesson plans for the following week. I made

I'M CHANGING

an effort not to bring work home." Mrs. Simmons smiled.

"I can understand that, but, Mrs. Simmons, I must say I was so surprised by your call about Tina taking her sister's purse. She is certainly going through some changes, but this progress report has me a little baffled."

Mrs. Simmons flipped through a thick folder. She found the page she was looking for and quickly read to herself silently. "Not a good progress report at all, but when you say surprised, what do you mean?"

"Looking at this progress report and knowing how smart Tina is, I'm shocked. Tina has always received good grades. She stayed on the honor roll in elementary school."

"You have to realize, Mrs. Morten, that middle school is a totally different place. These kids aren't used to the way we operate here. Tina is seriously struggling."

"Struggling?" Tina's mother had a puzzled look on her face.

"She's unorganized."

"I've noticed that, and that's why I brought her book bag. I want to know what she should and shouldn't have in her bag." Mrs. Morten lifted the heavy book bag and unzipped it.

"Is something wrong, Mrs. Morten?"

"Her bag is a mess." Tina's mother pulled out her student planner, loose, crumpled papers, thin folders, and a thick binder stuffed with papers. She looked at the bottom of Tina's book bag and saw pieces of M&M and Skittles candy, cookie crumbs, and loose paper clips. "I'm embarrassed," Mrs. Morten said, looking through Tina's belongings.

"Well, she only needs six thin pocket folders, writing utensils, her student planner, and her writing journal."

"She begged for this binder. I know it wasn't on the supply list, but she was going to have a major tantrum in the store if I didn't get it," Mrs. Morten said, shaking her head.

"That binder is one of many things that keeps Tina distracted."

"Tell me more please."

"She has this fancy pen with big purple feathers on the tip and clear liquid with glitter inside."

"Distracting, right?"

"Very distracting, but that's not all. She also has this gold glitter that she decorates all her papers with. Glitter is all on her desk, on the floor, on my desk, in my drawer." Mrs. Simmons laughed.

I'M CHANGING

"Some glitter ended up on my carpet at home. I don't know how, but it did."

"That glitter was supposed to be for art projects only. Oh boy."

"Well that's the thing we don't have any art projects that require glitter. She also has a key chain with all these charms and gadgets attached. The key chain wouldn't bother me if she kept it in her book bag, but when she swings it constantly, it's pretty loud."

"I told her to get rid of those things from her key chain. I know one of the charms has a little plastic jar—"

"—That she can blow bubbles from," Mrs. Simmons interrupted. "Oh yes, she demonstrated that for some of her classmates. Could you please get her to refrain from bringing these items to school?"

"Of course," Mrs. Morten said.

"I would also prefer if you tell her not to bring her electric pencil sharpener."

"She brought her Hello Kitty sharpener to school? That's for her bedroom."

"The class is quiet and students are working, and the next thing you know you hear Tina sharpening her pencils, and classmates' pencils."

"I'm listening to everything you're telling me, and I don't want this to come out wrong, but why didn't you warn me before?"

"I did."

"I never received any letters or calls home."

"You responded to all of my emails," Mrs. Simmons said.

"Mrs. Simmons, all of this information is new to me. I never received any emails I can promise you that."

Mrs. Simmons flipped pages in her binder. "According to my parent contact log, I emailed you on these dates," she said, showing her the form. "You emailed me back several times and said that you would talk to your daughter."

"Maybe you spoke to my husband, but he hates computers. Someone is up to no good. I'll get to the bottom of this," Mrs. Morten assured.

"I have two other things to give you as well," Mrs. Simmons said, going in her drawer. She took out Patrice's purse and Tina's student planner.

"Tina has two planners?"

"The planner you have in your hand is the new one. I have the old one. I found it under her desk."

"Wait, wait, this is too much. She has two planners?"

"She lost the old one, then purchased a new one."

Mrs. Morten shook her head. "Let me make sure I understand everything correctly. The planners are supposed to be signed daily right? I never signed the planners."

"I have your signature in here—look for yourself," Mrs. Simmons said, giving her the planner.

"This does look a lot like my signature. She's good," Tina's mother said, shaking her head in disbelief.

"So I guess you never saw this, either," Mrs. Simmons said, opening a manila file folder with Tina's name on it. She had copies of all the forms Mrs. Morten allegedly had signed but never received. Tina's mother read the forms.

STARLET REID

Dear Parent/Guardian of Tina Morten,

I am presently experiencing some problems with your child. I would greatly appreciate your cooperation in working with me on this matter.

The attitudes and behaviors below are very important to maintain stability within the classroom.

AREAS OF CONCERN

x Excessive Talking *x Disturbs others*
x Lack of Effort *x Does not complete work.*
x Not Prepared for Class *x Poor test scores*
x Inappropriate materials (toys, magazines, etc).

If you have any questions please call the main office to set up a personal conference.

Sincerely,
Mrs. V. Simmons

I'M CHANGING

Dear Parent/Guardian of Tina Morten:

We regret to inform you that Tina Morten is performing poorly in the following subjects; we would appreciate your help on this matter.

Math
Health

If you have any questions please contact us.
The sixth grade team

Mrs. Simmons gave Mrs. Morten another piece of wrinkled paper. "I also found this in the trash." The paper had bright capital letters that said "MISSING WORK." The sheet was filled with missing assignments. "You never saw this?"

"Never," Mrs. Morten said in disbelief. "I am so shocked. I never, ever had a problem out of her sister, Patrice."

"All kids are different."

Mrs. Morten rested her face in her hands. "It's my fault. I wasn't paying attention. What was I doing?"

"Trusting your daughter, that's all. Many parents believe their kids when they say they have no homework."

"I thought she was doing so well, but my sweet, innocent daughter has been a con artist. It doesn't help that she lost her best friend."

"I honestly think that Marci plays a very small role in Tina's performance. She likes Amanda Jo a lot. Listen, Mrs. Morten, you can't blame yourself."

"It's hard not to. Every day it's something different. I mean, she gets offended if I try to hug or kiss her. She constantly whines. 'My bread is too hard, my pillow is too fluffy,'" Mrs. Morten said, imitating her daughter.

I'M CHANGING

"Imagine having a class full of pre-teens," Mrs. Simmons said, smiling.

"That's why I praise you teachers. I couldn't do it. Having multiple Tina's in one class?"

"Trust me, I keep my headache medicine in my purse," Mrs. Simmons joked.

"All of this is mind-boggling. I mean, it's one thing to forge one signature, but this little lady not only committed forgery, but she went into my email account and committed fraud."

"Middle school is a critical time. These kids need to stay focused because in middle school that's when we begin to lose them. Their hormones are running wild and everything but work is appealing to them. You have to check the book bags on a daily basis, check the websites they're on, and keep the line of communication open."

"You're absolutely right."

"Tina is a smart girl who needs better study habits. I'm sure she can clean her act up. The good news for you is that our school website is being updated. Pretty soon you'll receive a special password. You'll be able to see all of Tina grades."

"I like that. She will improve, I promise. I just don't want to be too harsh. She really wants to try out for the cheerleading squad. Last year she didn't make the team."

"I know, Nancy told me," Mrs. Simmons said, smiling.

"I bet she did," Mrs. Morten said, laughing. "I know I should punish her, but maybe I can use the tryouts as an incentive for her to improve."

"That would straighten her out I'm sure."

Mrs. Morten exhaled slowly. "My daughter is changing right before my eyes. She doesn't need any more distractions."

"I totally agree with you on that," Mrs. Simmons said, closing her booklet.

"Now would not be the time to tell her that I'm pregnant."

Chapter 15

Tina never cried so much in her life. How did everything become so complicated? Her eyes were puffy and it felt like she had butterflies in her stomach. She paced back and forth in her room. What was Mrs. Simmons saying about her? She hoped she didn't mention the time she fell asleep in class. What if Mrs. Simmons showed her mother the *Bona Fide* story idea sheet that she confiscated? Her mother would be shocked to see some of the story ideas: How your cell phone can help you cheat on tests. Name your first teacher crush, and how to keep your enemies close. Tina looked at her blue cat clock on the wall; its eyes and tail moved side to side per second. Nothing was going the way she wanted it to. The boy she once loved now loved her old best friend. Her new best friend was mad at her. Amanda Jo was cool, but she wasn't Marci.

Tina missed Marci; she knew her better than anyone else. Marci was the only person who knew Tina passed gas on the school bus and blamed it on Daniel Tucker. Marci also knew about the antique vase Tina broke when she tripped over her shoestrings. Her mother paid three hundred dollars for the vase. Tina remembered blaming Jerry for breaking it. Marci would've never stopped talking to her because something didn't go her way like Amanda Jo did. She wondered if Amanda Jo was just as fake as Marci.

The phone rang, but Tina didn't answer it. She looked under her bed and grabbed her declaration of love folder dedicated to the one and only Christopher Edwards. Why did he have to be so cute? Why did he have to be so smart? *Did he laugh when Mrs. Simmons told me to take off my lip gloss? Does he really like Marci? Does he talk to Marci on the phone? Do they talk about me? What if they do talk about me? What if Christopher wants to take Marci to the Winter Dance? What if they stay a couple until high school graduation? What if they go to the prom together? What if they become homecoming king and queen? What if they get married?* Tina was going crazy thinking of the what ifs.

"Scooterbug," her mother yelled from downstairs.

I'M CHANGING

Tina jumped when she heard her mother's voice. She was back from talking to Mrs. Simmons. She didn't hear her mother pulling up in the garage. Tina peeked out her window. She saw her mother's car parked in the driveway. *Why didn't she park in the garage? Why is she being all sneaky? What did Momma know?*

"Come down here," she said. "Your father is on the phone." Tina felt numb. Tina really wanted to talk to her father, but what would he say? Tina slowly walked down the steps. Her mother sat on the sofa holding the cordless phone.

"After you get off the phone with your dad, we're going to have a nice, long talk," her mom said.

Tina gulped, then took the cordless phone from her mother. She sat beside her mother on the sofa.

"Hey, Daddy?"

"What's going on?" her father said. He was extremely loud.

Tina couldn't tell if he was upset. Was he going to extend her punishment? What did he know? Did he know about her stealing Patrice's purse? Would he confront her about the progress report? *Stay positive*, she told herself.

"Your mom told me that you've crossed to the other side."

"Crossed to the other side—what's that?" Tina said, looking at her mother.

Tina's mother laughed. "It means you're no longer an angel."

Tina's eyes welled up with tears; she put the phone closer to her face and whispered, "I'm your angel."

"Not lately," her mother said shaking her head.

"What's going on, Scooterbug?" her father said.

"I only told your dad about yesterday, not today," her mother whispered.

"What happened today?" her father asked.

"Well, Daddy, I want to talk to you in person, you know, sit on your lap and talk to you face to face," Tina said.

"You're getting heavy, Scooterbug, I think you're getting a little bit too big to be on my lap," he said, laughing.

Tina crossed her arms, held the phone up on her shoulders, and began to cry.

"Now, you need to stop all of that crying," her mother said.

Tina wondered if she was supposed to be talking to her father only because her mother continued to

I'M CHANGING

butt in. She wanted to tell her mother to be quiet, but she didn't want an Alabama butt whooping.

"What happened today?" her father asked.

Tina cried hysterically. She could feel mucus coming down her nose. Her head jerked as she tried to talk. "I-got-a-F-on-my-pro-gress-re-port," she said, sounding out her syllables.

"And," her mother said.

Tina began to cough. "I-took-Pa-tri-ce's-purse-to-school-with-out-asking-her?"

"And."

"Pa-trice-missed-her-field-trip-to-the-science-center-because-I-had-her-purse-and-every-body-hates-me-y'all-think-I'm-a-devil-now-and-not-an-ann-an-an-an-an-gel," Tina said, crying. She sounded like a broken speaker.

"You're right, Scooterbug, we're going to have to talk about this when I get home," her father said. "I love you, be good, and stay out of trouble."

Tina hung up the phone. Her mother wiped her tears with her thumbs. "I love you, Scooterbug."

"I love you too," Tina said.

"First of all I want to apologize for not being as active as I should have with your transition to middle school. I should've been there more, checking your work, signing your planner. I was distracted and for that I am deeply sorry."

Tina thought about what her mother was saying and she totally agreed. At Kellwagen her mother checked over everything, but ever since she started middle school her mother had given her more freedom.

"Scooterbug, you have been very, very dishonest. We did not raise you to be a liar—the emails, fake signatures, I can go on and on. What were you thinking? How long were you going to play charades? For heaven's sake, explain this behavior to me, young lady."

Tina cried, "I made a few mistakes, I'm not perfect. Middle school is just stupid." Her head continued to jerk as she cried. She tried to take control of her nerves, but she couldn't. "I just—just got caught up with the middle school lifestyle," Tina said, sniffing.

"This middle school lifestyle has you lying, forging my signature, talking back," her mother said. "Scooterbug, you never behaved like this, and to top it all off, you invited a total stranger to our home without consulting me or your father."

Tina interrupted, "Amanda Jo is not a stranger. She's my be-st friend, well, she was my best

I'M CHANGING

friend until—" Tina held back on her words.

"Until what?" her mother asked.

Tina took a deep breath.

"Until what, Tina Kaley Morten?"

Tina stopped crying. She took another deep breath and looked into her mother's eyes. "Until you told her she couldn't come over!" she said, raising her voice.

"This is what I'm talking about right here. Who do you think you're talking to? You really must be watching too many of those raunchy talk shows with the kids who talk back to their parents. I'm not into physical punishment, but you're making me think, you're seriously making me reconsider. Do not raise your voice at me, do you understand?"

"Are you going to give me an Alabama butt whopping?"

"What is an Alabama butt whopping? Patrice said something like that the other day."

Tina couldn't believe that her mother didn't know what an Alabama butt whopping was. There was no way she was going to explain it.

"You're so grounded, again. No computer, no phone, no going outside. Do you understand me?"

Tina nodded her head in agreement.

Chapter 16

The phone rang. *Thank you, thank you, thank you*, Tina thought. How she wished she were grown. Tina couldn't wait until she turned eighteen. She imagined her graduation day. She'd have her hair in big curls. Her lips would be a shiny pink shimmer. And she was going to wear a pretty dress with very high heels. Her graduation day would be the beginning of freedom. Tina couldn't wait for that day. No more washing dishes, folding laundry, cleaning the bathroom, taking the dog out, or watering the grass. *They're going to have to do it themselves.* A big smile covered Tina's face.

"Oh, you think this is funny?" her mother said, picking up the phone.

"No," Tina softly said.

"Shh," her mother said. "Hello…how are you? I'm sorry that Amanda Jo couldn't spend the night.

I'M CHANGING

Tina never asked for my permission. I was hoping to meet you first before they did any sleepovers… What?" her mother said in an alarmed voice. "No, she's not over here. You mean she didn't come home?"

Tina ran over to her mother, staring at her mouth.

"No, I told Tina to tell Amanda Jo that she couldn't come over," her mother said. "You did tell Amanda Jo, right?" her mother asked, putting the phone on her shoulder.

"Amanda Jo's not home?"

Her mother shook her head no and put the phone back to her ear. "I understand, I understand." She paused. "She never called you? Oh brother… Scooterbug," her mother said, looking at her, "Did Amanda Jo say she was going over to one of her friend's after school?"

"No, I'm her only friend," Tina said.

"Yes, I'll call around, please call me back… okay…bye," Tina's mother said, hanging up.

"She's missing?" Tina said.

"Yes, her mother was calling here to check on her."

Tina felt sick. It was entirely her mother's fault that Amanda Jo was missing. If she would've let

Amanda Jo stay the weekend, none of this would be happening. Tina hoped Amanda Jo was okay, but what if a stranger took her? What if Amanda Jo was so sad about not staying over that she hitchhiked a ride with a stranger? What if the stranger hurt her? What if Amanda Jo ran away from home and became a dancer who took off her clothes like that girl in the movie she and Patrice watched last week?

"Scooterbug, call some of your friends and see if they know anything," Tina's mother said.

Tina called everyone she could think of. Lauren told her that she saw Amanda Jo with Nancy, but she didn't believe her. Her mother called everyone in the neighborhood, but no one knew any additional information. Three hours went by, and they were the longest three hours of Tina's life. She cuddled in her mother's arms. Her mother looked really worried. Jerry licked Tina on the cheek, then tilted his head and looked at her. "Oh, Jerry, I hope Amanda Jo is okay." She hugged Jerry, then rubbed her hands against his soft fur.

Her mother got up from the sofa and started pacing; that's when Tina noticed that her mother had gained weight. *Taking all those naps and eating*

I'M CHANGING

will do that to a person, she said to herself. *She's walking back and forth because she probably feels really guilty about not letting Amanda Jo come over.* Tina began to get sleepy. She closed her eyes and quickly fell asleep. When she woke up the TV was on.

"Welcome to Channel 4 Nightbeat News. I'm Alison Freyton. A young girl by the name of Amanda Josephine Fields is missing. Amanda Jo, as her friends like to call her, was supposed to sleep over at a friend's house, but she never showed up. Leo Hayes has more of the story, Leo."

Leo stood in front of Linton Hall Middle School. He looked like a model with his good looks. "Thanks, Alison. I spoke with Amanda Jo's best friend, Tina Morten."

Tina couldn't believe her eyes, she was watching herself on the news. Leo held a microphone to her mouth, asking her all sorts of questions. The last question really triggered something. He asked her about her last conversation with Amanda Jo, and that's when Tina remembered something very important. She remembered that she never called Amanda Jo like her mother asked her to. She figured telling her in person would be better. Leo then said, "You waited until Friday afternoon to tell her that she couldn't spend the weekend over, didn't you?

Tina Morten, you're going to jail. You're going to be in so much trouble. HA HA." Leo laughed. Tina jumped out of her sleep and rubbed her eyes. She looked at the blank TV screen. Her breaths were short. She realized that she was just dreaming.

Her mother rubbed her leg. "It's getting pretty late, Scooterbug, maybe you should get ready for bed."

"You're right, Mom, good night," she said quickly.

Tina was nervous. One thing remained: Amanda Jo was still missing. There was no way she was going to share her revelation with her mother. A horn honked from outside, and Jerry barked. Tina and her mother quickly looked out the window. It was Patrice; LaToya's parents were dropping her off. Patrice walked in the house smelling like popcorn. She was happy and giggly until she saw Tina and her mother's faces.

"What's wrong?" Patrice slammed the door.

"Tina's friend Amanda Jo is missing."

Tina's mother recapped the whole incident to Patrice. Tina slowly walked up the stairs to her room. She plopped on her bed thinking about Amanda Jo. *I hope she's okay.* Tina closed her eyes and soon she fell asleep.

Chapter 17

Tina awakened to some voices she heard outside.

"We-are-the-champions. We-are-the-champions."

Tina stretched and looked over to Patrice's bed. She was asleep with her eye mask on her face. Tina didn't realize that she had fallen asleep in her clothes. She took a long stretch, rubbed her eyes, then looked at her clock: it was 12:32 a.m.

"We-are-the-champions."

Tina followed the voices. She opened her window and looked over to Nancy's backyard. Nancy was practicing her cheers with Marci and some girl.

Tina heard that laugh, hehehehehawhe. She rubbed her eyes. It was Amanda Jo! Was she dreaming? Tina pinched herself. She wasn't dreaming.

Tina quickly ran to her parents' room, but a sharp pain on her side made her hunch over. Tina held her side tightly.

"Ma," she yelled. "Momma."

Tina's mother came from her room, tying her robe.

"Amanda Jo is next door," she said, hunched over.

"You must be having a nightmare, honey," her mother said.

"She's next door, go look out my window," Tina said, pointing to her room.

"Why are you hunched over?"

"My stomach hurts. Mom, Amanda Jo is next door, go look outside my window," Tina said in pain.

Tina's mother heard the voices. She quickly went in Tina's room and opened the window. She called Amanda Jo's name.

Neighbors stood on their porches and sidewalks watching the reunion of Amanda Jo and her mother. Amanda Jo's mother pulled up to Nancy's house. Her hair was messy and she looked upset. Tina stood on the porch with Patrice and her mother. The cool wind brushed against her face. Amanda Jo and her mother hugged. Nancy's grandmother was babysitting since her parents were out of town. She had no idea that Nancy wasn't allowed to have company while her parents were away, but Nancy told her that her parents didn't mind. Trusting her granddaughter, she not only let the girls stay over, she took them to the mall and out to her favorite buffet.

"Thank goodness for a happy ending," Tina's mother said.

"I was worried sick over you," Amanda Jo's mother said, crying. "You were just piddling 'round, weren't you? Get your tail in that car!"

"Your friend is bad, Tina. I'm glad she didn't come over," Patrice said.

Tina was happy to know that Amanda Jo was safe, but watching her two former best friends stand in front of Nancy's house made her sick. Turns out Nancy invited Amanda Jo to her sleepover once she found out Amanda Jo had no place to go. Tina knew that she was the main subject of their get-together, and she knew they probably didn't have too many nice things to say about her. With her hurt feelings Tina went to her room and cried herself to sleep.

Chapter 18

When Tina awakened she felt a wet sensation between her legs. For the past three days Tina had noticed that her panties were wet, but she ignored it. Whenever her underwear became wet, she wiped the wetness away with tissue. Tina was too embarrassed to tell her mother her little secret. Her underwear felt as if it was filled with petroleum jelly. She didn't know what was going on.

Tina got out of bed and walked to the bathroom. She could hear Jerry's choke collar rattling and his little paws on the bathroom floor. Still half-sleep she sat on the toilet with her eyes closed and grabbed a handful of tissue. Once she was finished, she began to wipe in an upward motion.

"Hey, Jerry," Tina said, yawning. She opened her eyes and looked at the tissue in her hand.

I'M CHANGING

"Ahhhhhhhhhhhhhhhhhhhhh!" she screamed. She rubbed her eyes hoping that she was dreaming.

Her mother immediately ran to bathroom, tying the belt of her white terry cloth robe. She saw Tina sitting on the peach toilet.

"Is there a problem?" Patrice said, running in the restroom carrying a baseball bat.

"What's wrong, Scooterbug?" her mother asked, lifting her hair from her neck and twisting it into a ball. Jerry began to lick Patrice's leg. Tina said nothing. Her mother walked barefoot on the cold peach-and-black-tiled floor. Her scrawny eleven-year-old daughter didn't respond.

"Another bad dream?"

Tina looked up at her mother's slender, oval-shaped face. Her mother had a look of concern. Tina's lip began to shake.

"What's wrong, sweetie?" her mother asked again.

Whenever her mother made that face and said those words, Tina became weak and vulnerable. She began to cry in loud heaves.

Tina held up her soiled piece of tissue filled with red blood.

Patrice's eyes looked as if they were going to fall out of their sockets. Her mother smiled. "You started your period," she said in a shocked, but delightful tone.

Tina tried to recall where she heard that word *period* from. Then she remembered one of her health workshops. Ms. Hogan had showed some slides on the female reproductive system. Tina remembered thinking that the slides were gross, so she decided to write notes to Amanda Jo. Once the movie was over, Ms. Hogan turned on the lights.

"Starting your period is your introduction into womanhood. I hope the video provided you with the information you needed," Ms. Hogan said. "It's very important to know your body."

Tina couldn't believe that Ms. Hogan, the health teacher, was talking about periods. "Ms. Hogan is not the English teacher. I guess the next thing she'll talk about is question marks," Tina joked.

"You're only eleven and you started your period?" Patrice said, leaning against the towel rack shaking her head.

Tina shut her eyes tightly. Her body felt weird. What was happening?

"Help me," Tina yelled. "I'm bleeding to death."

I'M CHANGING

Patrice couldn't stop laughing.

"Patrice, stop laughing and put that bat up. Go and get your sister some fresh underwear out of her drawer and a pad out of the linen closet," her mother said.

"I can get a pad, but Tina doesn't own a clean pair of panties," Patrice joked.

"This is no time for jokes. Pads, panties, Patrice, please." Her mother laughed. "Okay, I couldn't help it. Did you notice the tongue twister? Oh never mind."

Tina tried to control the tears that came from her eyes.

"I'm sorry, sweetie," her mother said.

"What's a pad?"

"A pad will stop the blood from getting in your panties. They're also called sanitary napkins."

"So I'm going to keep bleeding?" Tina hesitantly asked.

Patrice entered the bathroom with a pair of panties that hung on the tip of a pencil. She carried a pad in her other hand. "These are the cleanest pair I could find. It took me awhile too," she said.

"Shut up," Tina cried.

"You need to start wiping your butt better," Patrice said.

"Alright, girls."

Tina looked at the lavender folded wrapper Patrice held in her hand. Patrice flicked the pair of panties off the pencil onto Tina's lap. Tina opened the wrapper and unfolded the long white pad.

"You're going to bleed for the rest of your life," Patrice said. "Bleed, bleed, and bleed."

Tina screamed.

"I'm going to have to go to the store and get you some regular pads. Patrice wears these super long extra absorbent maximum protection pads with wings," her mother said.

"Super pads?" Tina asked.

"She's a heavy bleeder," her mother said, rubbing Tina's hair.

"Heavy bleeding runs in the family, and your stomach is going to hurt like never before," Patrice exaggerated.

"Don't tell her that, Patrice," their mother said.

"I don't understand why she's acting so dumb. Like she doesn't know what a period is. You know what I went through."

"I don't pay attention to you!" Tina snapped. "I don't wake up every day and say, I wonder what

I'M CHANGING

Patrice is gonna do today. I wonder if Patrice started her period today. I wonder what Patrice is eating today. You're not special."

"Maybe if you did pay attention to me you wouldn't be sitting here right now having a Period 101 conversation."

"DON'T TALK TO ME!" Tina yelled.

"Girls, hush it up. Geesh and I wanted more—" Her mother stopped herself from revealing her pregnancy. "Scooterbug, every month you're going to have your period. You should have it the same time each month, but some girls and women have irregular periods."

"Mom, you're using big words. Remember you're talking to Tina. "Ir-re-gu-lar means not regular," Patrice said, sounding out the syllables to her sister.

"Don't be rude, Patrice, but your period will last for several days."

"Several days," Tina shouted. This had to be a bad dream. "Is a pad like a big bandage or something?"

Tina could tell that her mother wanted to laugh, but was holding it in.

"You're stupid, Tina," Patrice said.

"Fetch a bone," Tina snapped.

"Knock it off, girls," their mother said. "You're becoming a young woman, Scooterbug," she said, smiling proudly.

"Yeah and women don't play with toys anymore either, and they wipe their butts good," Patrice replied.

"Patrice, I can handle this," her mother said, giving Patrice a get-out-of-here look. Patrice stood by the bedroom door.

"Your body is going through changes now, honey. There's nothing to be afraid of," her mother said. "Oh my goodness, this explains some of your behavior. The mood swings and irritability."

"Irri-ta- what?" Tina asked.

"Mumph, mumph, mumph," Patrice said shaking her head. "Mom I told you you're using big words."

"Bye Patrice," her mother said. Patrice finally walked out the bathroom closing the door.

"You had PMS."

"What's that?"

"Premenstrual symptoms—some women are moody before they start their periods."

"Well, Patrice must have PMS all the time," Tina said.

"So your stomach really did hurt yesterday."

"Yeah, for the last few days, but you didn't believe me."

"I apologize, but you gave me a few good reasons not to believe you."

"So PMS changes some people?"

"It doesn't completely change them, but they may do things they normally wouldn't do."

Her mother continued talking about how her body was changing and what a period was. She talked about sanitation and other stuff, but whatever she was saying was a bunch of babble. Tina still didn't understand why blood was coming out of her body. The only thing she knew is that she wanted it to stop. She took a long warm shower. She didn't know how long she should wash down there. It felt very gross. She closed her eyes, sobbing heavily. This had to be the most painful experience of her eleven-year-old life. After she finished bathing, she turned off the faucet and squeezed her washcloth of excess water. She dried her body and put on lotion and powder. She slowly pulled up her panties, looking at the long, thick pad attached. It was very uncomfortable. Her thighs felt further apart as she walked with this big chunk of cotton between her legs. *I feel yucky,* she said to herself, *just yucky.*

Chapter 19

Later that morning Tina could hear the birds chirping outside her window, but she refused to get out of bed. She could hear the sounds of cabinets from the kitchen opening and closing. Tina heard someone pouring cereal into a glass bowl, the refrigerator door opening and closing, then Patrice's big mouth.

"Where is our new woman?" Patrice asked.

"Leave your sister alone," her mother said.

Tina lifted her body up, resting her elbows on her pillow. She tried to get out of bed to go to the bathroom, but her stomach cramped up. Tina decided that she wasn't getting up—it hurt too much.

Tina looked up at her white dusty ceiling fan, her mother opened her bedroom door, and Jerry hopped on her bed and sat beside her.

I'M CHANGING

"How's my little lady doing this morning?" her mother said, carrying a light blue laundry basket.

"I'm still sleepy," Tina lied.

"It's 9:30 a.m. on a Saturday morning and you're still sleepy?"

Tina watched her mother open the blinds, empty out the pink wicker clothes hamper, and sort the dirty laundry in less than five minutes. The aroma of sausage crept into Tina's room.

"Breakfast is ready, baby," her mother said, tugging at the pink comforter. "Get up, Scooterbug, I have to change your sheets."

"I'm not hungry," Tina said.

"Your stomach is still hurting?"

"Yes."

"Oh, my baby has cramps," her mother said in a baby voice.

"I'm staying in bed today." Tina sulked.

Her mother sat beside her and began to stroke Tina's hair. "Of course you want to stay in bed," she said. "You need to get up and walk around, but for now I'll leave you alone, remember, if you need anything just call my name." Tina's mother kissed her on the forehead and picked up the laundry basket exiting the room. Jerry followed her.

Tina began to cry. *Becoming a woman hurts*, she thought. *I don't wanna grow up.*

"Uhhhh, you're still crying?" Patrice said, entering the room and standing at the foot of Tina's bed. "There's no use in crying, it's only going to get worse. You saw those huge pads that I wear. I'm thinking of wearing tampons, though. You do know what tampons are, right? You stick them up your—"

"Shut up, Patrice."

Patrice's words hit Tina hard, and her body was filled with rage. *Why? Why? Why?* Tina thought. *Why is there blood coming out of my body?* She didn't understand.

"Hey, I'm just telling you like it is, honey."

Tina kicked Patrice on the leg. Patrice pulled the covers off of Tina making her scream. Patrice picked Tina up and spun around in a circle. Tina could feel the secretion coming from out of her private area.

"Stop, stop it, it's coming out!" Tina yelled, and the more she yelled, the more it came out. Patrice threw Tina on the bed and squeezed her breast. Tina hit her sister and folded her arms to protect her sensitive breast.

"Stop, that hurts," Tina said, crying. "You play too freaking much."

I'M CHANGING

Patrice laughed so hard that tears began to roll down her cheeks. Patrice put her hand on Tina's private and squeezed it then repeatedly said, "What's going on down there?" Patrice laughed hysterically.

Tina began hitting Patrice. "You make me sick. Leave me alone. Leave me alone!" she yelled.

"Hey, hey, hey, Patrice, leave your sister alone," her mother said, walking back in the room.

"She's a little crybaby," Patrice said.

"Be nice to your sister," her father said, peeking from behind the doorway.

"Daddy!"

Patrice hugged her father. Tina didn't want to get up.

Her father sat on the bed and hugged her.

"Tina started her period, Daddy," Patrice said. "And she's been crying all day. Big baby, I share a room with a big old baby. Lemme find your pacifier."

"No one made fun of you, Patrice, when you forgot to throw your used pad away a week ago," their father said.

"And remember, Jerry had the pad in his mouth," their mother added.

Tina began to laugh. "That's gross." She wiped her eyes.

"That wasn't funny, it was embarrassing. Aunt Shelia and Uncle Charles were over that day," Patrice remembered.

"Then Jerry ran downstairs with the soiled pad in his mouth. He hopped on Aunt Shelia's lap and tore all into the pad."

"That's when Uncle Charles held up the pad and asked, 'What's this?"

Everyone laughed except Patrice.

"You know what you have to do," their father said, looking at Patrice.

"Sorry, Tina," Patrice said, walking out of the room.

"Apology not accepted," Tina whispered.

"Scooterbug!"

"I was just kidding, Mom."

"This is what I've been talking about, honey. All this mouth," Tina's mom said to her dad.

Her mother sat down next to her husband and stared into Tina's big brown eyes. Tina could feel her eyes getting watery.

"Come on," her mother said. "What are you crying for?"

"It hurts, Mom," she said, sobbing heavily.

"Okay, time for me to go," Tina's dad said. "Let me unpack. I'll be back to talk to you,

Scooterbug," he said, kissing her. After he left, her mother touched her forehead.

"What do you mean it hurts? Do you mean it feels weird?"

"Yeah," Tina said, wiping her eyes. "Every time I stand up it comes out. Then Patrice ignorant butt squeezed my stuff and some more came out. I think I need to go change again."

"Let's talk about that. Patrice practically had a new pack of pads and I noticed that they're almost gone. You just started your period about two hours ago."

"I had to change."

"How many pads did you use in the last two hours?"

Tina closed her eyes and began to count the number of times she changed her pad. "I used about six."

"Six! Why so many?"

"Every time I feel it getting wet down there I change."

"Tina you're changing your pad too much. It's going to get wet down there, but don't change your pad every time you feel wetness."

Tina shook her head in agreement then she complained about having a headache.

"You really need to eat something. I'll bring you up something," her mother said, getting up.

"That will probably help. Can you pass me the remote? It's right there on the floor," Tina said, sniffing.

"No, you may have started your period, but you're still grounded," her mother said, standing by the bedroom door.

"But, Mom, I had PMS and when you have PMS you behave differently."

"PMS has nothing to do with poor grades, inviting company over without permission, and stealing your sister's belongings," her mother added. "And after what happened with your friend Amanda Jo..."

"Oh my goodness, you told me that PMS makes people do different things."

"You need to start taking responsibility for your actions. You devised a plan; it failed and now there are repercussions."

What the heck did she just say? Devised? What does that mean?

Her mother closed the door. Tina threw her pillow at the door and crossed her arms. "I've been stuck in this crummy room for days," she said. She poked out her lips, then clenched her

I'M CHANGING

fist. She could feel more blood secreting from her body, which made her cry.

She wondered what Amanda Jo was doing. She had to be in lots of trouble. Why did she go over to Nancy's? Was she part of a plot by Nancy and Marci to trick her into believing that Amanda Jo was really her friend? How could she go to school knowing that they played a practical joke on her? *All this drama in my life has to end,* Tina said to herself. She was never in trouble back in elementary. *Is this what the future holds? It's not my fault. I can't help it that everything around me is jacked up.*

Her mother opened the bedroom door halfway. The pillow Tina had thrown blocked the door. Her mother pushed the door open with her hip. She was carrying a tray of food.

"Throwing pillows?" her mother said. She placed the tray on Tina's bed.

"I was trying to make up—yeah, I threw the pillow," Tina said, deciding to tell the truth.

She stared at the scrambled eggs, sausage, and orange juice that adorned the tray. There was also a red velvet book with a lock on it.

"What's that book about?"

"I picked this up for you the other day, but I forgot to give it to you. It's a diary."

Tina eyes widened and a smile brightened her face.

"I never had a diary before," she said.

"I think this is a great way for you to express yourself instead of fighting with your sister and throwing pillows," her mother said, looking at the pillow on the floor.

"Thanks, Mom," she said. Maybe her mother wasn't so bad after all.

"This diary is one way to express yourself, but if you ever have a problem, I want you to know that you can always talk to your father and me."

"I love you, Mom," Tina said, kissing her mom on the cheek.

"And I love you back. I just can't believe how fast everything is happening. I mean, when I think about it, you had all the signs of a developing teen. Remember when we went shopping and I helped pull those tight pants off of you?"

"How can I forget?"

"You had lots of hair on your kitty patch."

"You call down there a kitty patch?" Tina laughed. "That's so lame."

"We were shopping for a bra…how could I be so blind?"

I'M CHANGING

"Mom, I'm sorry for everything. I really am. I promise, no more lies."

"I hope you're right."

"So let's talk about me joining the squad this year."

"Ouuuuuuuuuuuuuuuuuu," Patrice said, walking in.

"What's wrong?" Tina asked.

"G.O.S.S.I.P.," Patrice spelled.

"Is all of that necessary, Patrice?" her mother asked.

"I think you'll find this quite interesting, Mom, but before I begin let's back up to the night that Amanda Jo and her mother reunited. No one really questioned how Amanda Jo ended up hanging out with Nancy. We were all just so happy that Amanda Jo was safe."

"What is this leading to?" their mother asked.

"Well, the truth is about to be revealed. I just got off the phone with Beverly, who lives on Northshore Drive, the same street as Amanda Jo. Anyway, she told me that Amanda Jo never got a phone call from your darling little Tina about not being able to sleep over. Let me repeat that. Tina never, ever called Amanda Jo to tell her that she couldn't sleep over. And it's so true, Mom, because if you remember that day when Tina was supposed to call Amanda Jo, Tina got in trouble and she stayed in her room and fell asleep early. That was the same night Daddy left for North Carolina. When did Tina have time to call Amanda Jo? That's the million-dollar question," Patrice said, smiling.

Tina was numb. Just when things were working out, Patrice had to open her big mouth.

"Scooterbug told me that she called Amanda Jo, right, Scooter?" her mother asked.

"She's a liar, Mom. Hasn't she proved how much of a liar she is these days? The planners, forged signatures—I can continue, but we don't have all day. To conclude, everyone was worried about Amanda Jo all because Tina didn't tell the truth. And guess what else, Mom?"

"I don't think I want to know."

"Now this is just pitiful; apparently Tina told Amanda Jo that she couldn't come over on Friday during fourth period! Or was it after fourth period? Amanda Jo brought her bags to school and everything, but it gets better, Mom, it gets better. Amanda Jo had nowhere to go because her mother was out to dinner. She didn't know what to do, and that's when red-pepper next door invited her to come over."

I'M CHANGING

"That makes a lot of sense," Tina's mother said. "Amanda Jo's mother still should've called me to get consent or tried to meet me before allowing her daughter to come over. There is no way you two could go over to a friend's and I don't know the parents."

"You have to remember, Mom, they're country, they think everyone has good intentions," Patrice said.

"Is any of this true, Scooterbug?" her mother asked.

"What part?"

"Tell me the truth."

"Well, somehow, some way, somewhere along the line, Amanda Jo didn't get my message until Friday um, um, at the end of fourth hour," Tina said in a low voice.

"What am I going to do with you Scooter?" her mother said.

"What are we going to do?" Patrice said, shaking her head.

Tina's mom walked out of the bedroom. Tina cut her eyes to Patrice and frowned. "You talk too much and you get on my nerves."

"I am so happy I'm moving out of this room," Patrice said, stretching.

"Where are you going?"

"I convinced Mom and Dad to make the den my new room."

"Why can't I have the den and you stay up here?"

"When you lie, steal, tamper with email, forge documents, and start your period before you're twelve, bad things happen," Patrice said, walking out of the room.

Tina ate her meal and when she finished, she slowly walked over to lock her bedroom door. She hated getting up because she could feel more blood flowing to her pad. She picked up her diary and walked over to her window and looked outside. Nancy's backyard was empty. Tina sat in the window nook and began to write in her diary.

Dear Diary,

Something horrible happened to me this morning. I started my period. I don't know why they call it a period because the blood won't stop coming out of my body. They need to call it a comma, that's what I'm going to call it. I'm on my comma. Who made up the word period for this mess that comes out of my stuff? I wish it would stop, like a

I'M CHANGING

period should, but it doesn't. I can scream. I feel so nasty and mushy. Everything on my body is sore. Why is this happening to me? Why now?

Everyone makes me so sick. Shadow is fake and I wish that she was never my best friend. Shadow and Pepperstank can have each other. Amanda Jo is a two-faced sellout. She's lucky I even noticed that she existed with her grits-mixed-with-eggs-butt. Pepperstank needs to find her own friends with her dry red hair. How dare Amanda Jo go over to her house? I can even accept if she went over to Chante's, but Pepperstank?

My mom believes everything that comes out of Patrice's stupid mouth. Patrice is so rude. I don't care if she moves to the family room. Bye! Good riddance! Won't lose any sleep! Daddy said I'm getting too big to sit on his lap. I don't want to sit on his fat leg no more anyway!!!!

Tina's bottom lip began to shake. She put her head in her diary and began to cry.

Chapter 20

Tina took a deep breath. She realized that in the last few days all she had done was cry and complain. She took another long, warm shower and put on a new outfit. Her mother allowed her to sit on the front porch for some fresh air.

Tina opened the screen door and stood on the porch. The neighborhood was pretty quiet. Mrs. Roberts from across the street was watering her flowers. Nancy rode her bike from one corner to the other. Once she saw Tina on the porch she started to ride her bike with no hands.

Tina sat on the big white swing that hung on their porch. She watched a bee circle the bushes. That bee didn't have a worry in the world, Tina thought.

"There you are," Tina's father said, opening the screen door. Her father wasn't fat at all she

I'M CHANGING

thought. She really looked at her dad. He is kind of cute to be old.

"If I'm not mistaken you're not supposed to be out here," her father said.

"Momma said I could get some fresh air. She said I needed it."

Her father sat next to her. He smiled at her and kissed her on the cheek. "Talk to me, Scooterbug, what's going on?"

I started my comma, a duh, Tina wanted to say. What did he expect her to say? *Why do adults ask stupid questions?*

"Your mom told me about your moodiness and about your friend Amanda Jo."

"Well, Daddy, I really don't know what to say. I made a few mistakes and now I'm paying the ultimate price."

"How?"

"I'm bleeding, trust me, this is a bad punishment."

"You can blame Eve for that. It's something all girls go through, and boys go through things also."

"They don't have commas, Daddy, well, periods, so you really can't compare."

"Okay, you got me on that one. I'm getting all of these reports from your mother about your behavior; it sounds like you can't adapt to change."

"Sure can't. I want everything to stay the same."

"I got some bad news for you, Scooterbug. One of the things about life is that things always change."

"I wish they didn't. I wish I was back at Kellwagen. I had so much fun."

"Middle school isn't that bad, is it?"

"Yes it is, everybody acts so stuck up and goofy; they're constantly trying to be like other people instead of being themselves. They think they have to wear what other people are wearing to be liked and that's not true. Like one day you can be best friends for years, then all of a sudden the little redhead girl takes your friend."

"Sounds like you don't like middle school because you're not friends with Marci anymore."

"I don't care about her skinny, big-nosed, fake—"

Her father interrupted her. "Scooter."

"Well, she is skinny and her nose is too big for her face, but," Tina's voice began to shake. She shrugged her shoulders, "She doesn't want to be my friend anymore. I didn't do anything

I'M CHANGING

different. I stayed true to myself, but it wasn't good enough."

"Friends come and go and you'll find out that your real friend is the girl you see in the mirror and your sister."

"Patrice?"

"I know you can't visualize it now, but it's true. If Marci was a real friend she'd still be your friend. You don't want a fake person in your life, do you?"

Tina smiled. "No I don't. It just hurts a little bit and it's not just Shadow, I mean, Marci. Amanda Jo did the same thing too. Pepperst—Nancy is always getting people on her side."

"The only thing you can do is stay true to yourself and if Marci or Amanda Jo don't like it, then you're better off without them."

"It's easier said than done. I share classes with them."

"Speaking of classes, explain your progress report to me."

"I just think, well, I really think I wasn't focused. I thought that middle school would be so cool, but I always pictured myself with Marci, and seeing her be best friends with Pepperst—Nancy really hurt my feelings."

"Why do you keep saying Pepper, then Nancy's name?"

"I kinda made up a nickname for her. Her last name is Pepperdine as you know, but her attitude is stank so I just call her Pepperstank."

Tina's father laughed, but he told her that it wasn't nice having mean nicknames for people. Tina agreed, but that nickname defined Nancy, and she was going to be Pepperstank forever.

"But back to my grades, I'm not trying to make excuses, but art helped me release some stress," Tina said.

"You have time to bring your grades up, but an F in health?"

"Health is boring."

"You learn about the proper foods to eat and your body, right?"

"Yeah."

"And according to Patrice you didn't even know what a period was."

"Patrice needs to shut up!"

"Scooterbug, be nice. Why is health boring?" her father asked. "Don't blame it on Marci."

"I just have to get focused. I like the health workshops and I like working on our magazine, *Bona Fide*, the magazine I created."

I'M CHANGING

"I'm aware, I'm aware," he said.

"Everything is just hard. We have to read all the time, and I don't know if I can do it," Tina whined.

"When you started Kellwagen you were scared, but then you adjusted. You started middle school and you were scared and you're adjusting; then you have to start high school, then you have to start college, then you have to start a new job. Then you're going to get married, move into a new home, have children. Life is about changing and adjusting."

"Dang Daddy, you just put my whole life out there," she laughed. "Daddy, I'm about to tell you something that may shock you, but I don't want to grow up," Tina pouted.

"I don't want to see an F on your report card. You have no choice but to grow up and to improve in your classes. Get it together, Scooterbug," her father said, getting up and kissing her on the forehead.

"I promise that I'll try," Tina said. Her father opened the screen door with a big smile on his face.

"And, Daddy, could you please start calling me Tina? Scooterbug is getting just as old as I am."

Chapter 21

Sunday was a nightmare for Tina, she experienced more cramps. Her mother put a heating pad against her stomach. Tina stayed in bed for the rest of the day. If Sunday was a nightmare for Tina, Monday would be her biggest challenge. She had to go to school.

Tina walked hunched over, carrying her books. Amanda Jo closed her locker and noticed how tired Tina looked.

"Hold your horses," Amanda Jo said.

Tina didn't hear Amanda Jo and continued to walk. She grabbed Tina by the arm and Tina dropped her books.

"Sorry," Amanda Jo said, picking up Tina's books. "I'm sorry about going over to Nancy's." When she looked up she saw the biggest pimple on Tina's cheek—a big red pimple with a white spot in the middle.

"I don't feel good," Tina complained.

"I can see that, I mean you look very tired," Amanda Jo corrected herself. Tina rolled her eyes at Amanda Jo. Students quickly exited the hallway. Everyone stared at Amanda Jo when she walked in. Mrs. Simmons took attendance while students did their bell work.

"Good morning, class," Mrs. Simmons said. "After what happened with Amanda Jo this weekend, the principal suggested I talk to you guys about responsible behavior."

"Amanda Jo gave us quite a scare," Louis said.

"Indeed, Louis," Mrs. Simmons said. "Students, we can learn a lot from what happened with Amanda Jo. Never make plans without consulting your parents or guardians."

Mr. Baylor knocked on the classroom door. Mrs. Simmons walked out in the hall to talk to him. The class took it upon themselves to have their own discussion.

"Amanda Jo, my mother even prayed for your safe return," Dawson Banks said.

"A lot of people were worried for nothing because Amanda Jo was hanging out with Nancy," Chante said.

Everyone in the class looked at Nancy.

"I thought Amanda Jo called her mother," Nancy snapped. "You guys need to be patting me on the back. Amanda Jo would've been roaming the streets. She already looks homeless."

The class made sounds to egg on an argument.

"Don't make me come over there and whoop your tail," Amanda Jo said. "I thought we had fun," she said to Nancy.

"You call listening to the cricket's fun? Yes, AJ wanted to listen to the crickets because it reminded her of Old Sweet Tennessee. Well, newsflash, this is the city, not some dirt back country road called Hickory Lane. There's no sitting by a pond wearing overalls in the big city, honey," Nancy snapped.

"Ouuuuu," the class said.

"Like listening to you brag truly makes the sun shine. You try to be so uppity, but I know your secret."

"What secret?" Nancy said.

"The books you stole your ideas from."

"What are you talking about?"

"You do travel, I'll give you that, but you make up what happens on your trips," Amanda Jo said.

"How do you know she makes things up?" Louis McDougal asked.

"Because when she took her thirty-minute shower, I got bored. I looked on her bookshelf and I saw these books called *The Adventures of Little Earl and Bucky*."

"Close your mouth right now," Nancy warned.

"Who the heck is Little Earl and Bucky?" Ace asked.

"They're popular young adult books overseas. Nancy has the boxed set," Amanda Jo said. "Tina, remember when you told me that story about Nancy being stuck in some country and they cut her hair and sold it? Well, Little Earl is the one whose hair was sold, not Pepperstank."

"Don't you ever call me that name, you hear me?" Nancy demanded. Her face was red as a beet.

"Pepperstank, Pepperstank, Pepperstank," Amanda Jo repeated.

"You have the exclusive boxed set of *The Adventures of Little Earl and Bucky*? Can I borrow some of your books?" Louis said.

Mrs. Simmons walked in the class and closed the door. "Where were we, class?"

"Mrs. Simmons, you just missed some good stuff while you were out in the hallway." Chante smiled.

"It was like watching my soaps," Ace said.

"Let's focus, class. I have a question. Amanda Jo, how did you end up over at Nancy's when you were supposed to be at Tina's?" Mrs. Simmons asked.

"Originally I was supposed to go over to Tina's, but she told me at the last minute that I couldn't come over. Nancy overheard what happened and then invited me over."

"The problem is you never called your mother. Students, always communicate with your parents. Remember, you're still a child and you can't do what you want to do when you want to. End of discussion."

Tina doodled in her notebook. The cramps reemerged and her pimple was killing her. She put her head down and wondered why she didn't stay home for the day.

"Tina, please sit up," Mrs. Simmons requested.

Tina could hear her classmates laughing. She slowly lifted her body; then she heard a loud gasp from the class.

"Gross," Chante said in disgust. "Your pimple busted all over your notebook."

Tina looked down at her notebook and saw blood. She ran out of the classroom crying. She

I'M CHANGING

quickly ran toward the girl's restroom, but she bumped into Ms. Hogan.

"Hey, slow down," Ms. Hogan said, grabbing Tina by the arm. "Tina Morten, what's wrong?"

Tina didn't want to tell anyone about her period, especially Ms. Hogan. "I have to go to the bathroom,"

"Crying like this?" Ms. Hogan said.

Tina nodded her head yes, then went inside the restroom and grabbed some tissue from one of the stalls. She slowly walked over to the mirror, staring at her busted pimple. She wiped her tears, then wet the tissue and dabbed it on her pimple. She turned off the water and looked at herself in the mirror. She felt uncomfortable and sloppy. Her clothes felt like they were on too tight. She held the sink tightly; she could feel moisture coming out of her body and onto her pad. Her life had been turned upside down. She felt like she was no longer in control.

There is no way I'm walking back in that classroom. Tina threw the tissue away and looked at herself again in the mirror. She heard adult voices in the hall. She adjusted her clothing; then she analyzed her busted pimple. Maybe she could sneak into the library. Tina waited for the voices to disappear and then she slowly walked out of the restroom.

"Tina," Ms. Hogan said, standing in the hall, "What's going on?"

Tina was startled by her presence. "My pimple busted in front of everyone."

"Mrs. Simmons told me that you were also sleeping in class. She thought that it would be a great idea for you to come back to my classroom with me."

Tina really didn't want to go to Ms. Hogan's class, but she definitely didn't want to go back to her class. Maybe Ms. Hogan had some treats to give to her, but what if she told her that the F she had on her progress report would also appear on her report card? After listing the pros and cons in her head, she decided to go to Ms. Hogan's class.

Posters of the food pyramid, body structure, getting proper rest, and exercising filled the walls of the empty classroom. Ms. Hogan closed her classroom door. Tina sat at the front table.

"It feels a little different sitting up here instead of being at the back table, huh?"

"Yeah, it does."

Ms. Hogan sat across from Tina. Her hair almost looked orange. She looked a little sleepy

I'M CHANGING

Tina found herself staring at her teacher's freckles.

"So what's going on, Tina?"

Tina remained quiet.

"Now you want to be quiet. You're never quiet in my class."

"My pimple busted on my cheek. I had this big pimple on my cheek—well, it's not big now because it busted, but it was. It really did hurt, the pimple, it did," Tina rambled.

Ms. Hogan gave Tina a small round bandage to put on her pimple.

"How old are you, Tina?"

"I'm eleven."

"I remember when I was eleven. It's a rough time. You're trying to figure out who you are, who you want to be, who you want to be around, and in addition your body is going through changes. Have you started your period?"

Tina was dumbfounded. How did she know? *Am I walking funny? Can she see my pad through my pants? Can she smell me?* Her stomach started bubbling. *Please don't let out a big one.*

"Yes, Saturday morning I started," Tina said. "But I don't call it a period, I call it a comma. If there's one thing I learned early on in life it's that red means stop, you know, like stop signs. A period means the end, as in no more, so it makes more sense to say comma, because when you have a comma you have to pause. The blood stops, then starts, stops, then starts it's like on pause. What I'm trying to say is it just doesn't make sense to use the word period," Tina rationalized. "I've been on my comma for three days now."

"Those three days can extend to a week."

"A week!"

"Let me try to speak in your terms. You'll know when your 'comma' is about to be a period. Your flow won't be as heavy. Very interesting the whole using comma opposed to period. Anyway I pretty much figured that you started."

"How?"

"The pimple, the sleeping," Ms. Hogan said, smiling.

Tina couldn't believe that Ms. Hogan knew. One of her teachers knew that she was on her comma…could life get any more embarrassing? Tina thought to herself.

"Believe it or not I used to be a preteen. Well, I actually started my comma when I was fourteen," Ms. Hogan said, smiling.

"Did you have PMS?"

I'M CHANGING

"No, I never had PMS, but I know people who do."

"Why does the blood come out of our body?"

"Don't you remember the movies we watched in health class?"

"Uggh, what movies?" Tina asked.

Ms. Hogan walked to the green chalkboard and drew a picture of a uterus. "Your period takes place in your reproductive system. Do you see these round circles?" Ms. Hogan said, pointing to the picture on the board. "These are called your ovaries and your ovaries contain thousands of eggs. One egg is released each month, and this egg travels along your fallopian tubes. Do you see these yellow marks?" Ms. Hogan colored on the female reproductive system with a piece of yellow chalk. "Once your ovary releases an egg, this yellow part begins to get really thick in your uterus, and this thick blood lining called the endometrial leaves your body through your vagina. This is the blood that you see, so, Tina, this in essence is how you get your comma. Do you understand now?"

Tina looked at the picture on the board. "So this thing is in my body?"

"Yes, Tina."

"Why don't boys get commas?"

Ms. Hogan leaned against the wall and took a deep breath.

"Well, forget the boys for a minute, but my boobies hurt. Why?"

"Boobies?"

"Yeah my tata's, my bee beeps, hooters, doorknobs…they're sore."

"Come again?"

"My breasts hurt."

"Oh, your boobies, tata's, hooters, and doorknobs are your breasts. You're right people do call them, those things you mentioned. Anyway some women experience PMS, sensitive breasts, acne, cramps and backaches during their periods. Some girls even get sick and throw up. All of this is pretty normal and it goes away within a day or two or maybe stays throughout the period."

"Is all of this part of puberty?"

"Not just puberty grown women go through this as well. Do you remember when we talked about the changes that happen during puberty?"

"You mean growing hair and stuff?"

"Right. During puberty you're no longer the cutie you used to be, nor are you blossomed enough as a teenager; you're in the middle. I like to

I'M CHANGING

call it metamorphosis. Your body is going through some major growing pains. Take a look at some of your friends. Look at their height, facial hair, the sound of their voices. The other part of puberty is called adolescence, and in adolescence many things are tested; friendships, your relationships with your parents and siblings make you sick. You're trying to find yourself. There are constant questions like, Will I ever be popular? How can I fit in with others? Do people like me? It's growing pains at its best," Ms. Hogan said. "Does any of this sound familiar?"

"Yes," Tina said with a smile. She finally had an explanation about what was happening not only to her body, but what was happening in her life. She was growing up. She was turning into a young woman.

"I'm going to ask you something really personal, Tina, but I need you to tell me the truth."

Tina gulped.

"How do you wipe yourself when you go to the restroom?"

"When I do number one or number two?"

"Number one," Ms. Hogan said, smiling.

Tina laughed. "Well, I take the tissue and wipe."

"Are you wiping up or down?"

"Up."

"You're wiping the wrong way. Always wipe down, then drop the tissue in the toilet."

"Why?"

"If you wipe up you can cause bacteria to spread, and this can cause an infection. It's very sensitive down there," Ms. Hogan said turning red.

"Can I use powder down there?"

"Perfumed soap and powders can irritate some people, so stick to non-perfumed items if you can."

"We need to do a story in *Bona Fide* about this."

"That's a good idea. You can write the article, but I'll have to approve it since I am the editor in chief." Ms. Hogan smiled.

"Who appointed you editor in chief? I mean, you're the editor in chief?"

"Who else would be the editor in chief?"

Me. I should be the editor in chief. It was my idea, duh. "Thank you, Ms. Hogan," Tina said, getting up. "That's a lot of stuff to remember. I really appreciate the time you took out of your schedule to explain this to me."

I'M CHANGING

"Please sit back down. We need to discuss why you're failing my class."

After her talk with Ms. Hogan, Tina walked back to Mrs. Simmons' class. As she walked to her seat, she looked at her classmates and noticed how different everyone looked compared to last year. Amelia Hall's teeth were bigger, Curtis Carpenter had sideburns and peach fuzz above his lips, Cameron Jackson had to be a foot taller, Daniel Tucker stunk even more, and Chante Baker's mouth had gotten bigger if that's even possible. Everyone was going through puberty, that's when Tina realized she wasn't alone.

Chapter 22

Tina was starving; she took huge bites out of her ham sandwich. Amanda Jo sat next to her in the lunchroom, but she was still mad at her for going over to Nancy's house. She didn't know how to act towards Amanda Jo. Should she be friendly? Was she supposed to forget her friend's betrayal?

She was really happy about her conversation with Ms. Hogan. Everything made sense. It really was time for her to start over, to let go of the past, and improve. Tina made mental notes to herself about studying more and cleaning her room.

"How did you get that big pimple?" Daniel Tucker asked.

"How did you get that big stomach?" Tina said.

I'M CHANGING

"I was just asking a question; you didn't have to get all mean."

"There is a way to ask someone a question without being rude."

"Okay, how's this? That big red thing on your face that you're covering up with a bandage, how'd it get there?"

"I'm eating right now," Tina said, biting into her apple.

"What'cha lookin' at?" Lauren asked Louis.

"I'm trying to figure out," Louis said, "Is it Lauren or a dog. Oh, it's Lauren the dog."

"I know you're not talking about people, Louis, with your clumsy self," Chante interrupted.

"Spell clumsy," Louis said to Chante.

"No."

"Because you can't spell," Louis joked.

"I can," Chante said. "K L."

Everyone at the table laughed. Chante rolled her eyes and drank her chocolate milk.

"I'm too mad at you right now," Ace said, eating his yogurt.

"Well, I know how to spell clumsy," Amanda Jo said.

"Good, now spell toothpaste cuz you need some," Louis snapped.

The table laughed hysterically.

"Guess what? Remember our old substitute teacher back at Kellwagen, Mr. Armstrong? I saw him at the mall on Saturday. He had on a short-sleeved shirt and a big tattoo on his arm. By the way, Marci, he was wearing butt chokers and high heels," Joseph Alexander joked.

"No he wasn't," Marci said.

"You still have a crush on Mr. Armstrong?" Tina said to Marci. The table started to laugh.

"Do you still have a crush on Christopher Edwards?" Marci asked.

Everyone looked at Christopher.

"She can have a crush on me," Christopher said with salad dressing on his face.

Tina's heart melted. Did he really mean it?

"So I guess you like flat-chested girls, huh, Christopher?" Nancy said.

"I used to like you," Christopher joked.

Tina wished she had a camera for Nancy's reaction. The table laughed.

"Well, I'm not flat-chested anymore," Nancy rebutted.

"You call those mosquito bites breasts?" Christopher said.

The table laughed so loud that Ms. Caldwell,

I'M CHANGING

the cafeteria assistant, wrote the class up and they couldn't have PE for the rest of the week.

Mrs. Simmons was very upset with the class as they returned from lunch. "It has come to my attention that there has been a lot of name-calling going around. This needs to stop because name-calling can turn into bullying. We have zero tolerance here at Linton Hall for bullying. Everyone has feelings. You don't like it when people talk about you, so stop talking about others. Name-calling is truly a middle school epidemic."

"Spell epidemic, Chante," Louis whispered.

"You aren't listening, Louis. Why are you picking on Chante?" Mrs. Simmons asked.

"Because, Mrs. Simmons, you should be able to spell words like wait, behave, friends, and clumsy in the sixth grade. Now illiteracy, that's another epidemic."

Louis always managed to squirm himself out of getting in trouble. "I only make fun of Chante to encourage her to go home and practice her spelling, but my reverse psychology hasn't worked."

"Chante, how do you feel when Louis talks about you?" Mrs. Simmons asked.

Chante organized the papers on her desk acting as if she were busy.

"Chante?"

"I don't care about his stupid butt," Chante yelled.

"Stupid, no." Louis put his pointy finger up. "Four point oh with honors, *toots*!"

"Louis, there is nothing wrong with being smart and confident, but there is no need to be arrogant and demeaning," Mrs. Simmons said.

"Point taken. Showing that I am mature, let me extend my apology to you, Chante," Louis said, taking a bow.

Tina smiled. Louis was funny. He always made her laugh.

"Very good, Louis." Mrs. Simmons smiled. "Do you accept his apology, Chante?"

"If he meant it," Chante snapped.

"Mademoiselle, pardon moi," Louis said.

"He makes me so sick," Chante said.

"Louis, apologize," Mrs. Simmons instructed.

"Sorry, Chante," he said.

"Don't worry, TeTe," Ace whispered to Chante, "I'm gonna help you on your spelling,

I'M CHANGING

okay?" Chante smiled at Ace and they gave each other a high-five.

"Everybody already know that spelling is my weakness," Chante said. "But let me remind you Louis that I always place number one in Math and Science. Who called me yesterday trying to figure out our Math formula huh? You're scraggly butt comes in third all the time behind Marci it's been that way since Kellwagen so don't act brand new."

"Scraggly butt Chante?" Mrs. Simmons said shaking her head. "Class, if anyone is caught name-calling you'll be assigned detention for two weeks." The dismissal bell rang and Tina hurried to her locker.

Dear Diary,

I was so embarrassed in school today. My pimple busted on my notebook in homeroom, in front of everyone!!!!! Like my worse moment in school ever behind throwing up on Mrs. Tye-Allen in first grade. I ran to the restroom crying. I didn't want to come out. Ms. Hogan took me to her class and she told me lots of important things like how to wipe myself properly and what happens to your body during your comma. I think momma tried to tell me all of this stuff the day I started my comma, but I was too spazzed out to pay attention.

Shadow is still fake and so is Amanda Jo. Hummm Amanda Jo needs a nickname maybe: Hehaw—for her laugh—or Blondilocks—because of her hair. I'll have to think about that one.

Anyway Amanda Jo hurt my feelings. She did the same thing Shadow did to me. I thought I really had two good friends, but like daddy said life is about changing and adjusting. Forget them!

Louis is so cute. He went off on Chante Baker today and it was so funny. I just don't get it Chante is so smart when it comes to math and science, but give her a word to spell the girl can't do it. Maybe if she stopped being so nosey and practiced her spelling she could improve, but that's just like asking Marci not to take huge bites out of Pepperstank's butt—not gonna happen!

My stupid comma is almost over and I'm really excited about trying out for the cheer

I'M CHANGING

squad. Mom helps me organize my book bag and she checks over all of my assignments. Momma + Daddy said that I could try out for the squad, but if my grades don't improve I mind as well forget about it. You know I'm not having that. Well I better start practicing, tryouts begin on Wednesday. Let me rephrase that, I better study then practice for the squad. See I'm already improving!

Tina studied all of her subjects, even math, and when she was done she practiced her routine for the squad. Her biggest challenge was doing a cartwheel; every time she attempted to flip, she froze. The thought of flipping her body over was scary. She sat on top of her radio and began to think about last year when she didn't make the squad. She felt humiliated and Nancy didn't make the situation any better. Tina believed that she didn't make the team because she couldn't do a cartwheel. She knew that she had to overcome this fear. She stood up, turned on her radio, and practiced her routine over and over. After hours of freezing up on her cartwheels Tina eventually began to do half flips.

Chapter 23

Later that evening Tina sat on her bed and combed her doll's hair. Patrice was moving her items to the den. Tina couldn't wait to have the room to herself.

"You can't take that," Tina argued.

"This is my radio that Mom gave me for my birthday, so be quiet."

"I'm glad you're leaving."

"Likewise," Patrice unplugged her radio. Tina watched her sister put the radio by the door.

"Stop looking at me. I know you're going to miss me."

"Whatever." Tina continued to comb her doll's hair.

"I'm so glad I don't have to listen to your stomach roar and listen to you snore while you're asleep."

I'M CHANGING

"I'm glad I don't have to wake up and see dried-up drool on your face." Tina laughed.

Patrice sat on Tina's bed. "Well if I'm being honest—"

"You, honest? Ha!"

"I'll miss you a little bit. We've been roomies all our lives. Remember when it used to rain and you would get in my bed with me? You were so scared of the lightning."

"And you would sing to me."

"Until you fell asleep."

"How did I end up in my bed in the morning?"

"I carried you to your bed. You used to fart as I carried you over too."

"Did not. Remember the fights we had in this room?"

"There were so many. They all ended in the same—you crying."

"I think I might miss you," Tina said, looking over at her sister.

"Don't get all sentimental on me," Patrice said, getting up. "Let me tell you something. I have been meaning to have this talk with you now that you're on your period, exclamation point, apostrophe, or whatever you call it. You need to know a few things about staying fresh. First, you need to have period panties; those would be the panties you only wear during your period. Usually they're the ugliest panties you have, but in your case that's all of your panties. Secondly, you need a calendar to keep up with the days you have your period, and last, but certainly not least, you need a hygiene kit to take to school."

"What's a hygiene kit?"

"You would ask that, wouldn't you? A hygiene kit is an emergency kit to take to school with you in case of accidents or funkiness."

"What's in a hygiene kit?"

"Deodorant, wipes, pads, panties, toothbrush, toothpaste, mouthwash, and dental floss. Trust me, you'll need it, and keep an extra outfit just in case in your locker."

"Mom needs to take me shopping then," Tina said, standing up.

Patrice reached for her radio. "Well, that's my last piece of advice to you."

"You act like you're going off to college. You're only going to the family room."

"You know, Tina, you're like a baby, still got milk behind the ears. I'm not only going to the family room; this is a new phase in my life."

I'M CHANGING

"Okay, I've heard enough. Get out of my room," Tina said, standing by the door.

"Make me." Patrice put the radio on the floor.

Chapter 24

Tina sat on the bleachers in the gym with the other sixth-grade cheerleading hopefuls. She watched as each girl flipped, stomped, clapped, and cheered. Nancy was up next. She wore a cute cheerleading outfit with pompoms to match. Her long red hair was pinned in a ball. She stood in the middle of the gym with her back facing the crowd.

"Are you ready?" Nancy yelled as she did a backwards flip. Everyone clapped. Nancy started off really good, but she made the mistake of trying to dance. She was totally off rhythm. She was dancing too fast. This was unexpected because Nancy usually had more rhythm. As she concluded her cheer, she did the splits halfway and held her pompoms in the air. Tina couldn't believe how poorly Nancy did.

I'M CHANGING

"Thank you, Miss Pepperdine," Ms. Gillard said, writing something on her clipboard.

Nancy sat down feeling confident. Tina's stomach bubbled; she was nervous. She was next.

"Tina Morten," Ms. Gillard, said looking at the sixth-grade hopefuls.

"Here I am," Tina said, getting up.

"Show me what you got," Ms. Gillard said.

Tina cheered as if her life depended on it. Each step was concise. She told herself not to think about the next move. She let her body naturally flow. She spun and then she did a handstand. She landed back on her feet and began to kick with passion. She ran, then did a full cartwheel. The crowd clapped as she landed with her hands on her hips. She couldn't believe it—she actually did a cartwheel. Tina chanted over and over:

Get the spirit
Let it go
When you do
Lose control

"Thank you, Tina," Ms. Gillard said.

Tina was so happy with her performance that she skipped all the way back to the bleachers.

"That was real cute, but watch and learn, baby, watch and learn," Chante said, walking past Tina. She couldn't believe her eyes; Chante had a different hairstyle. Her thick hair was in one ponytail. It looked like she got it pressed or flat-ironed. She wore a short black skirt and a white T-shirt with an ice cream cone on it. Chante took her position. She took a deep breath, then began.

I'm better than you
I'm bet-ter than you
Watch my moves

Chante began to dance like a professional. She did back flips, cartwheels, and the splits.

I'm better than you
I'm bet-ter than you
Watch my moves

Chante yelled her cheer. Tina never saw Chante so focused. She put her hands on her hips. The crowd went wild, but just when everyone thought she was done, she began to step like a

I'M CHANGING

sorority girl. She tapped her knees, lifted her legs, and tapped the heel of her feet with her hands. Then she started to dance, with so much energy it looked like her body was about to break.

"I'm better than you, I'm better than you," she yelled with her hands pointing toward the onlookers. Everyone stood up and clapped, the first and only standing ovation. Chante ran back to the bleachers and sat next to Tina.

"Oh my God, you were so awesome," Tina said, hugging Chante.

Chante took heavy breaths as she fixed her socks. "I know, you took notes, right?"

Tina shook her head and laughed. Chante smiled at her. "You were okay too, Morten," she said.

Tina began to get really nervous. Would there be room for her on the squad? Chante was by far the best. What if Ms. Gillard forgot all about her performance? These were questions she wanted the answers to. After watching the other sixth-grade girls do their routine, Ms. Gillard told the ladies to change back to their school clothes in the locker room. Everyone in the locker room praised Chante.

"Good job too, Morten," Jessica McKay of 6-3 said.

"Thanks," Tina said, reaching in her book bag. She was very nervous, but excited. She could feel blood coming out of her body. Maybe it was time to change her pad. *When is this comma going to go away?* Tina asked herself. Then she remembered her mother telling her that when you're excited or have physical activities, fresh blood may come out. As she reached inside of her book bag to take out her hygiene kit, everything spilled on the floor.

"Let me help you," Amanda Jo said, bending down. "What in the hot crackling lard is this?" she said loudly, holding up Tina's lavender sanitary napkin wrapper.

"It's my pad, silly," Tina said, snatching it.

"Pad! You started your period," Nancy said loudly.

All the girls in the locker room surrounded Tina and bombarded her with questions, and she loved all of the attention.

"How does it feel?"

"Does it hurt?"

"Do you wear tampons?"

"Is it messy?"

"First of all, I don't call it a period, I call it a comma, because the blood just doesn't stop," Tina said.

I'M CHANGING

"You got that right," Khesha Jenkins of 8-1 said. "I like that. A period should be called a comma!" Khesha quickly made up a song: *My comma, my comma keeps going and going, the blood, my blood is flowing and flowing.*" She repeated the phrase and someone added some hand claps, and soon the whole locker room was rocking to the song. Once the jam session ended more questions ensued.

"Why do you have all of this stuff in that pouch?" Chante said.

"It's called a hygiene kit. Since we're getting older we have to protect ourselves from body odor. I have some moist wipes in case my underarms smell. I also have trial-size deodorant, powder, toothbrush, toothpaste, mouthwash, and dental floss. Oh yeah, I also bring an extra pair of panties."

"Wow, you have all of that?"

"It's better to be safe than funky," Tina said, putting the items in her pouch.

"I'm going to get me a hygiene kit," one of the girls said.

"Hey, maybe we all can get together and get Daniel Tucker a kit," another girl said. Everyone laughed.

"Remember, no name-calling," Marci said.

"But Daniel does stink," one girl said.

As the girls changed their clothes, Marci walked over to Tina.

"I always thought I'd get my period before you," Marci said.

"Well, I always thought we'd be best friends," Tina said, zipping her pouch.

Marci rolled her eyes and attempted to walk away, but Tina had more to say.

"I just need to understand why. What did I ever do to you?"

"What are you talking about?"

"Our friendship, that's what," Tina said with her hand on her hip.

"Nancy's not that bad."

"But you had to stop being my friend altogether. You completely cut me off."

"I tried to talk to you, but you just won't listen. I'm sorry," Marci said.

"That's it, you're sorry? After all these years you're just sorry? I loved you like a sister, probably more than my real sister. We had some good times."

"We did, but things change, Tina."

"No, people change," Tina said, putting her book bag on her right shoulder. "I just never

I'M CHANGING

thought you would." She said walking out of the gym.

If Amanda Jo and Shadow want to be Pepperstank followers, well, fine, Tina said to herself, *but I'd rather be alone any day than to be around fake wannabe's.*

"Tina, Tina," Chante yelled. She put her book bag on her back. "Wait up."

"Who did your hair?" Tina asked as Chante walked next to her.

"You're not gonna believe who did my hair."

"Who?"

"Ace."

"Ace knows how to flat-iron?" Tina asked.

"Girl, he can do a full set of spirals with a flat-iron."

"How long did it take to get your hair so straight?"

"About an hour."

"Were you scared?"

"A little, but once he showed me his slideshow of previous customers, I was sold." The girls walked out of the gym together.

"Wait up, wait for me," Amanda Jo said, running toward them.

"Don't try to hang around us because we're the best cheerleaders," Chante said.

"I'm not," Amanda Jo said.

"I don't know if I'm going to be able to get along with you, Chante," Tina said.

"Why not? You're bossy, I'm bossy at least we're not some wimps."

"You just talk a lot of junk," Tina said. "Yeah I found that little note you wrote about me being fake."

"Well you were being fake trying to wear lip gloss and eye shadow. You looked silly. Well the lip gloss was cute, but the eye shadow made you look cheap. We're only in the sixth grade we got plenty of time for all of that. Plus you know I speak my mind. Life is too short to keep quiet and be a follower," Chante said, looking at Amanda Jo.

"Whatever," Amanda Jo replied.

"I'm just saying, I'm not easily persuaded like others," Chante said shaking her head at Amanda Jo. "Anyway Morten, why did you and Marci stop being friends again?"

"We just grew apart, okay? You are extremely nosey." Tina laughed.

"I just want to know what went down, that's all, and I'll get the truth, you bets believe that, but anyway you started your comma," Chante said.

I'M CHANGING

"It's about time. I've been on mine."

"For how long?" Tina asked.

"About two months," Chante said.

"Did it hurt when you started?" Tina inquired.

"Oh my goodness, I thought I was going to die when I started mine," Chante said.

"How does it feel?" Amanda Jo asked.

"You haven't started?" Tina said.

Tina and Chante began to laugh, but then they both told their stories about entering womanhood.

Chapter 25

F riday morning the cheerleading results were posted.

6th

Baker, Chante
Fields, Amanda Josephine
Franklin, Kianda
Knight, Krystal
Morten, Tina
Sanchez, Maria
Wang, Marci

7th

Chatman, JaNai
DuVal, Jeanee
Evans, Turkesia
Morrow, Khemberly

Reid, Savannah
Roulhac, Tiffany
Sims, Dawn
Williams, Stephanie

8th
Frett, Tami
Jenkins, Khesha
Lopez, Jamila
Mason, Heather
O'Conner, Bethaney
Weathersby, Yolanda
White, Vertna

Tina couldn't believe her eyes when she saw her name posted. "I made it, I made it!" she screamed.

"Me too," Marci said. The girls were so excited they hugged each other. "Your routine was cool," Marci said. They stared at each other and smiled.

"Everyone who tried out, thank you," Ms. Gillard said. "Those of you who did make it, meet me five minutes after school for further details."

"There must be a mistake," Nancy said, pulling Ms. Gillard's arm.

"Ms. Gillard, you can give Nancy my spot if you want to," Marci said.

Tina was outraged by Marci's behavior. She was actually going to give up her spot on the squad for Pepperstank? She took a deep breath and she refused to let Marci or Nancy rain on her parade.

Chapter 26

"I made the squad, I made the squad," Tina said, running in the kitchen.

Patrice was sitting at the table with LaToya eating snacks. "How did you make it? You have two left feet," she said, walking toward Tina. "This is going to be comedy at its greatest."

"Have you ever smelled tuna mixed with sour milk?" Tina asked.

"No, that's gross," Patrice said.

"Please stand back because that's what your breath smells like," Tina said, smiling.

LaToya laughed quietly.

"I'm gonna give you your moment—now shoot, you fly."

Tina searched the house for her mother. She found her upstairs talking on the phone in her room. She gently knocked on the door.

"Okay, I'll talk to you later, okay? Bye," Tina's mother said, hanging up the phone. "What happened? I heard you yelling."

"I made the squad, Mom," she said, hugging her mom.

"Well, good for you. Guess who I just spoke to?"

"Who?"

"Ms. Hogan—she said that you're improving."

"She did?" Tina smiled and starting singing. "Everything is working out. I can scream and I can shout! Everything is working out that's what I'm talking about."

"I'm proud of you."

"I have a question, though. Why didn't you tell Dad about the emails and fake signatures?"

"What makes you think I didn't tell him?"

"Because I'm still alive."

"Your dad knows."

"What? I don't understand."

"I ran into your classmate Joseph Alexander's mom at the grocery store. She told me about this great punishment she gave her son last year."

"Joseph just got off that punishment this year!"

"Exactly."

I'M CHANGING

"I'm going to be on a punishment for a year?" Tina whined.

"Let's not call it a punishment; let's call it probation. You did some really bad things, Scooterbug, and until all your grades go up we're going to be watching you. You violated our trust and for that you'll have to pay the price. I'm also gonna have Holly's Baker's daughter help you with your math. She's going to be your math tutor."

"Chante?" Tina crossed her arms and poked out her lips.

"Come here," her mother said, hugging her. "Look at you, you're getting so big," she said, rubbing Tina's hair. "You're getting tall, growing bosoms, got hair on your kitty patch…"

"Mom!" Tina blushed.

"And starting your comma."

"But I'm still the baby," Tina pouted.

"Well, not for long," her mother said, rubbing her stomach.

Tina frowned at her mother.

"You're going to be a big sister," her mother said.

"Eww, you and Daddy, eww," Tina said, frowning. She covered her mouth like she was going to hurl.

"Are you happy?"

"I guess. I think it will be pretty cool having a little sister," Tina said.

"Or brother." Her mother laughed.

Tina began to imagine having a little sister. She thought about the pretty dresses her new little sister would wear. Tina pictured cute ribbons in her hair and the cute accessories she'd wear. Her new little sister would be a replica of herself, her own real-life doll. Her new sister was going to do whatever she said. Tina remembered how much she adored Patrice when she was younger. The thought of adoring Patrice was actually a gross thought now.

Chapter 27

The family went out to TGI Friday's for dinner to celebrate her mother's pregnancy and Tina making the squad. Patrice's friend LaToya joined them for dinner.

"Order whatever you want," Tina's dad said.

"Tonight is all about me and Mom." Tina smiled.

"Well, it won't be once Mom has the baby." Patrice smiled.

"Don't say that," their mother said.

"It's true, honey, you won't be the baby anymore," Tina's father said.

"I am eleven years old. I'm almost a teenager! I don't care about being the middle child."

"We'll see," Patrice teased.

"You act just like a seventh grader."

"You cry just like a second grader," Patrice replied.

"Okay, girls, settle down," their father said.

Tina smiled as she sat at the dinner table. *This time next year I'll be feeding my baby sister.* She thought about the baby's fat cheeks and her cute little pigtails. She looked at her parents and realized that she was a lucky girl. She began to think about being on the squad, getting her uniform, performing in front of the crowd. She actually overcame her fear of doing a stupid cartwheel. Pepperstank didn't even make the team. Tina began to laugh.

"What's so funny, honey?" her mom asked.

"I was just thinking about everything, how lucky I am." Tina smiled.

"You certainly are," her dad said.

Everyone was stuffed after dinner. Tina couldn't even think about dessert.

"That was so good," Patrice said, belching.

"Patrice, where are your manners?" her mother asked.

"She never had any," Tina said.

"Be quiet," Patrice said.

"And we're having more kids?" their father said, looking at their mother.

"You said *kids*, Daddy. This isn't going to be the last one?" Patrice asked.

I'M CHANGING

Their parents looked at each other, then smiled.

"Come on now, this has to be the last kid," Tina said, making her eyes big.

"Well, I guess it's time to tell them," Tina's mom said.

"Tell us what?" Patrice said, making her voice louder.

"Well, your mom is further along in her pregnancy."

"Huh?" Tina said.

"We didn't want to say anything until we knew for sure that everything would be okay."

"Everything is okay, isn't it?" Patrice asked.

"More than okay," their father said, smiling. "You guys don't know, but we've been seeing a fertility specialist."

"A who?" Tina asked.

"A fertility doctor helps parents conceive a child," her mom said.

"Huh?" Tina said again.

"Oh my goodness, you are so challenged!" Patrice snapped.

"Patrice!" her dad said.

"Well, she is."

LaToya laughed as she sipped her water.

"Tina, honey," Patrice said. "Sometimes a mommy and daddy have difficulties, let me rephrase that, they have complications—no, that word is too big for you—they have problems making a baby, and a fertility doctor helps them."

"Patrice is right, fertility doctors do help, and my doctor did help me. When you're successful with fertility drugs—"

"You took drugs!" Tina interrupted.

"Oh my goodness!" Patrice said, outraged by Tina's naivety.

"The drug, which is the medicine, called fertility treatments helped me get pregnant."

"Huh?" Tina didn't understand anything they were saying.

Everyone sat at the table quietly and stared at Tina.

"Now you wonder why we argue," Patrice said. "Do you know if it's a boy or a girl?"

"It's a girl," Tina said.

"Sometimes when fertility drugs are successful, the mother can have multiple births."

"Hold up, I get it now. Like that lady who had eight babies, the Octo-Mom. Are you having eight babies?"

I'M CHANGING

"Absolutely not! But I can tell you this much: we're not having just one baby," their mother said.

The girls screamed in excitement.

"Two little sisters!" Tina laughed. "Oh my goodness, oh my goodness, oh my goodness!"

"Hold up, girls," their father said. He held their mother's hand. "There's something else."

Tina and Patrice were so excited that they didn't hear their father. They jumped out of their chairs and even hugged each other. Their parents gave them a few minutes to calm down.

"Okay, girls, we're really going to need your help with the babies."

"Do you know what you're having?" Patrice said.

"Yes, we do."

Tina was so excited, "Twin sisters! Oh my gosh! Oh my gosh! Oh my gosh!"

"Scooterbug, you're going to love the babies regardless."

"Okay, one baby can be a boy, but as long as I have a little sister, my world is GOOOOOD," Tina sang. She laughed loudly and clapped her hands together. "Twins, twins, twins." She stood on her chair and announced to the whole restaurant that her mother was having twins. Everyone in the restaurant clapped.

"Thank you," their parents said, nodding their heads at the crowd.

"Scooterbug, sit down," her father said.

After doing a few more dances Tina eventually sat down. She sipped some water from her glass.

"You are so embarrassing," Patrice said, covering her face.

"She's just excited," their mother said. "You're going to be excellent big sisters, but, Scooterbug, I'm afraid that the babies are boys."

Tina spit the water out of her mouth. "Boys!"

"I'm going to ignore what she just did," Patrice said, wiping her arm with her napkin.

"Congratulations," LaToya said, smiling. "I'll help baby-sit."

Tina sat with her mouth open. Water dripped down her chin. She couldn't believe it. "Two brothers? Are you sure?"

"Well, we're sure about the boys, but—"

Tina's eyes brightened; maybe her parents were playing a practical joke.

"But, I'm not having twins," their mother said. "We're having triplets."

"Triplets!" Tina said.

I'M CHANGING

LaToya and Patrice cheered in excitement. Patrice hugged her parents.

"All boys, are you sure? There's got to be a girl somewhere in the mix," Tina said, wiping the water from her chin.

"We have two beautiful girls already. Now we have to make room for your brothers."

"Brothers!" Tina said. She could feel her breaths becoming shorter. She could feel her eyes watering.

"I can't believe it, I am so excited. I'm going to have three baby brothers!" Patrice smiled. "Let's order some dessert."

"Sounds good to me," their father said. "Tina, do you want some dessert too?"

Tina was in a state of shock about the babies. "Wait a minute, you called me Tina, instead of Scooterbug."

"Well, you are getting older and you're about to become a big sister. Remember what you told me about 'Scooterbug' getting kind of old," he said, winking at her.

Tina's bottom lip began to shake.

"Here we go," Patrice said, shaking her head.

Tina began to cry. Everything was hitting her at once. Not only was her mother having a little boy, but three little boys, no new sisters, no cute dresses, no ribbons. Tina's imagination began to run wild. Three little boys jumping on her bed. Three little boys running around the house. Three little boys playing with their goofy trucks and hard action figures. Three little boys, dressed like boys. All boys. Three boys. No girls.

"It's not fair," she cried. "Everything was going so good and now this? I can't breathe, I can't breathe," she said, wiping her eyes.

"Wipe your tears," her father demanded. "Your brothers are blessings. You're going to be a big sister. Sit up straight and get your act together right now."

Tina's head jerked as she fought the tears. She knew that her father meant business. If it was up to her she would sit under the table and cry her eyes out, but she knew she couldn't do that. She took a deep breath and looked at her mother. She apologized for her tantrum.

Dear Diary,

Guess what? I made the cheer team, but we'll get back to me in a minute. I have other news to report and this bites big time. My mom is having triplets, all boys!!! I should be happy, but why couldn't one be a girl? It's so unfair.

I'M CHANGING

I cried. I think I'm going to cry later tonight too. Thing is my mom has been pregnant for months. I knew she was getting fatter. She's always saying, talk to me, tell me what's on your mind, be honest. Like hello, follow your own advice. She's been pregnant for four months and kept it a secret. See, parents say one thing and then do another. Oh and she did tell me PMS changes people. I am not crazy. I know what she told me, and then she wants to change her mind when it makes sense to her. I know one thing; I'm not babysitting three rock-headed boys. I'm about to be 12 too. Shoot I have a life!

    Anyway back to the best topic ever, me. I'm so proud of myself for making the squad. Pepperstank didn't even make the team. I kinda feel bad for her...OVER IT, ha! Chante was the best. Her hair was pretty today. It's about time she got a new hairstyle. She is trying to be my friend. I don't know if it's going to work out, but I'll give her a chance. Amanda Jo is trying to come back into the picture too. Mom said she could sleep over in a few weeks. It's going to be weird having someone besides Shadow sleeping over.

Chapter 28

For someone who had low self-esteem and declared that she was fat and ugly, Lauren was a total diva for her photo shoot for *Bona Fide*. Everyone thought she would be shy and very self-conscious, but they were wrong. Lauren showed up to Mrs. Pepperdine's photography studio wearing sunglasses and talking on her cell phone. Ace walked behind her carrying a big tote bag. Chante carried her outfits.

As the assistant editor in chief, Tina was at the studio to choose the best cover shot. Mrs. Pepperdine's assistant was present, and because Nancy was supposed to catch a flight with her mom after the shoot, she was there also.

"Wow, Lauren, you look great. Your hair is amazing," Tina said.

"You know I had to work my magic," Ace said, sorting through his tote bag.

I'M CHANGING

"Thanks, sweetie," Lauren said, kissing Tina on the cheek.

Lauren walked over to Mrs. Pepperdine and they talked about various shots she wanted to take. Chante pulled Tina's arm and whispered in her ear, "Girl, it's amazing what a flat-iron and some lip gloss can do for a person. She thinks she's in Hollywood."

"So what are you, her personal assistant?"

"Something like that," Chante said, hanging Lauren's clothes. "*Mumph,* I see that your girl Nancy is here. Let's go over there and say hi."

Nancy stood by the water cooler playing with a hand-held game. Tina was very apprehensive about talking to her enemy, but she decided to be mature. It was going to take every rational bone in her body to be civil to Nancy. Ace called Chante's name, but she pretended as if she didn't hear him.

"Chante, get over here. We need your help."

Chante was torn—she wanted to help Ace, but she didn't want to miss out on the conversation between Nancy and Tina. She looked at Ace; then she turned her head back to Nancy and Tina. She repeated looking back and forth until Ace snapped his finger and demanded her presence. Chante was so desperate not to miss any gossip that she asked Tina to go with her, but she declined.

"What game are you playing?" Tina asked Nancy.

"I'm not playing any games. You're the one coming over toward me acting suspicious."

"I meant what game are you playing." Tina pointed at the game in her hand. "You shouldn't be so paranoid."

"Like I'm going to take advice from you. The same girl who abandons her friends when they're in need."

"What do you mean abandon? What happened with Amanda Jo was—"

"Foul, it was foul," Nancy interrupted. "You left your friend hanging and I was there as usual to pick up the pieces."

"Okay, you want credit for saving Amanda Jo from the Boogie Man on the streets? Okay." Tina started to clap. "But that's all the credit you're going to get from me."

"Typical Tina, never wanting to take responsibility for her actions. Face facts, you abandoned Amanda Jo and Marci."

"You got that twisted. Marci started hanging with you; she dumped me."

"Do you know what your nickname is? *Mirror,* because everything is about you."

"About me?" Tina couldn't believe the nerve of Nancy, trying to blame her for the demise of her friendship with Marci.

On the other side of the studio, Chante wrapped a scarf that was supposed to be for Lauren's neck around her face. She was too preoccupied with the heated discussion taking place by the water cooler. She wondered what they were saying. She decided to work really fast so that she could find out what was going on.

"Someone has amnesia seriously. Think, Mirror that day I invited you both over for manicures."

"You came over to show off that bra." Tina filled a cup of water, then took a few sips.

"True, but I was tired of us fighting. I mean, we're neighbors. I made the first step. Marci was cool with the idea, but not you."

"Right, she abandoned me."

"No, she didn't. When she came over that day, all she talked about was you. Actually that's all she ever really talked about, *Tina likes this, Tina likes that, I remember the time when Tina…* I never told her to stop talking to you."

"Like I'm supposed to believe that." Tina tossed her empty Styrofoam cup in the recycle bin.

"Marci tried to reach out to you so many times, and you just shut her down. All those excuses you gave that girl about calling were bold-face lies. You never returned her calls. She had the audacity to cry over you." Nancy was determined to tell Tina the whole truth and nothing but the truth. "I was tired of her being depressed over you. I kept telling her to be positive."

Tina laughed, then looked over at Lauren posing for the camera. Ace turned the radio on and started to dance. Tina began to snap her fingers to the beat until Nancy told her to pay attention.

"On the first day of school, Marci couldn't wait to see you, but here you were with Amanda Jo. She complimented your hairstyle and you know what you told her? You told her to fly a kite! When we got off the bus, she spoke to you, but you had an attitude. She even pretended to like Christopher Edwards to get your attention. The bottom line is you were mad at her for being friends with me plain and simple. She finally saw the light that Tina Mirror Morten only cares about one person and one person only—herself."

I'M CHANGING

Tina couldn't deny Nancy's accusations; it was as if someone hit her in the head with a blow dryer. She closed her eyes and tried to retract everything that Nancy had said. She took short breaths and all the memories flooded back. Nancy really did invite them both over. Tina did lie to Marci about calling her, but never did. She thought about the times she pretended to have a stomach ache when Marci would knock on the front door to visit her. She thought about how rude and moody she was toward Marci last summer up until now. She questioned herself, why was she being so mean? She opened her eyes and saw Nancy staring at her with her hands on her hips. At that moment she knew the answer. She didn't want to share Marci, especially not with Pepperstank. The truth was Marci didn't change...*she* did.

An hour had passed. Everyone circled around Mrs. Pepperdine as she went through Lauren's photos on her digital camera. They finally decided on the cover photo.

"I look so pretty," Lauren said, smiling at her photo. "I just have a few more requests."

"No to the third power. We tired of you, Miss Thang," Ace said.

"I'm not asking you, Miss Thang," Lauren snapped back.

"Well, don't ask me for any favors," Chante said. "Don't even look at me. I am so mad at you."

"For what?" Lauren asked.

Chante rolled her eyes and stood in her infamous stance. "You made me miss out on the best piece of gossip ever."

"Sorry, but this request is not for you either, it's for Mrs. Pepperdine and her assistant. Can y'all airbrush my arms, thighs, and stomach? *Please*," Lauren said in a baby voice.

Chapter 29

Tina sat on her bed and opened her diary. Jerry nestled his body beside her. She put her diary down and picked him up. She looked into his big black eyes. She tried to make eye contact, but he only wanted to lick her face.

"Jerry, these last couple of months have been *woof woof woof*," Tina laughed. "You get it? Rough, these last couple of months have been rough, but you know what? No matter how bad it's been, you've always been there for me. You don't judge me at all and I love you for it." Tina kissed her puppy. She leaned back in her bed. Jerry licked her leg and fell asleep next to her. She grabbed a pen and opened her diary.

Dear Diary,
This is going to be a long entry because

STARLET REID

I have a lot to tell you. The good news is that everyone likes Bona Fide, but the bad news is Lauren. She heard some boys making fun of her on the cover and she started to cry. She's still mad that Mrs. Pepperdine didn't airbrush her like she asked. We kept telling her Bona Fide means real, like keeping it real, like being yourself. She really thought she was gonna be airbrushed, that's why she came to the photo shoot like she was a celebrity. What part of NOT GONNA AIRBRUSH didn't she understand?

Lauren doesn't like the way she looks. There is nothing wrong with that girl. She's actually really fun to be around and she has the prettiest smile like ever! She needs to be herself and stop worrying about other people. I guess I really can't talk about anyone because I'm still trying to figure out who the heck I am.

It's crazy because Lauren never talked about the way she looked until we started middle school, and I never had this much drama in my life since middle school. Maybe it's safe to say that middle school kinda sucks! But I'm getting my act together just like my folks said. They got me on probation and out of all people Chante is gonna be my math tutor! I bet she can't wait to come over.

Momma checks my book bag all the time. Now I gotta start hiding my snacks somewhere else. Parents just don't understand we need those snacks to give us energy. I still think it's dumb to have a student planner too. Why do my parents have to sign my work? This is junior high! The teachers are always saying you're older, be responsible, but we still need our parents' signatures. What kind of sense does that make? I'll tell you NONE!

My hand is starting to hurt from all of this writing, but I have no choice momma said I can't make any online videos. Plus she said kids these days use the computer too much. Talking about we need to go back to the days when handwriting was important. What year is she living in? She's lucky my handwriting is cute.

Pepperstank sat up there and gave me the nickname Mirror. Maybe she's on to something. I'm talking crazy now, but maybe I

STARLET REID

have been thinking about myself and putting my needs before others. What's so wrong about that? I mean shouldn't I put myself first? Me and Marci were a team, as in just us two. No Pepper and no Stank was part of our friendship. I just don't know if I can bring myself to like Stankilicious, ha ha I just keep coming up with the best nicknames. You know what I just realized about myself? I think I might be a little selfish.

PepperStank is trying to be nice. Could I possibly be friends with her? Marci and Amanda Jo like her so she can't be that bad, right? I mean, she's a show off, a friend snatcher, and thinks she's all that and a bag of chips, but... maybe, possibly, perhaps I could, sort of, kinda, search deep down, way down, like below, underneath, peel the layers from the darkest depths of my soul and let go of the past and find a warm place in my heart and be her friend.

I got a confession to make for your eyes only. This isn't an easy thing for me to admit, but here it goes...I'm the one that caused all the drama. I'm not proud of it either. I just wanted things to stay the

I'M CHANGING

same. I guess as you get older things do change, like my grades, like my attitude, like my body. Remember my first bra that was a 32B? Do you know I'm now a 34C? If I keep growing this fast I'm gonna be wearing a triple D by the 7th grade! Amanda Jo was right—life is like a hairstyle; curly, kinky, straight, and frizzy. Sometimes my life feels like a bad perm. Hold up, that doesn't even make sense! Let me think about it... Life is like a hairstyle, meaning life is always changing? Okay I get it now!!! Amanda Jo is so smart, but she has to be to hang with me.

From now on I'm going to be a lot nicer, a better student, a better friend, and most of all a better person.

OMG my hand hurts... So all this time Marci wanted to be friends! I still don't like how she was gonna give her spot on the squad to the Stankster, and I'm still mad at her for hugging up on my man. Marci is just, maybe she's about to start her comma. Maybe that's why she's acting different. OMG she probably has PMS. I don't care about that though I just know that I miss her so, so, so, so much.

I don't know how I'm going to apologize to her. I have been thinking about that all day. Should I call her? Should I visit her? Should I bring her a gift? Do I start off apologizing and then give her a gift? Maybe I can find a song that expresses how I really feel and tell her to listen to the lyrics. Maybe I can type the lyrics out and print it on yellow paper. That's it—yellow is Marci's favorite color. I'll print the lyrics and then I'll decorate it with butterflies and hearts. I'm gonna have to beg my momma to let me use my glitter. I hope Marci forgives me. What if she doesn't? What if she hates me the same way I hated Pepperstank? What if she shreds the beautiful yellow decorated paper I'm going to give her? If she shreds that letter that I took the time to decorate with my pretty gold glitter she can forget ever, ever, ever being my best friend again. I don't waste my glitter on silly stuff. I don't know what to do. What should I do?

The only thing that I do know is that I'm ready to start over. I can't wait until second semester.

<End>

I'm Changing Reading Questions

1. Why was Tina nervous about starting Middle School?
2. How did Marci and Nancy become friends? How did this make Tina feel?
3. Amanda Jo quickly became Tina's new best friend; do you think Tina used her to make Marci jealous?
4. Why do you think Tina was rude to Marci throughout the book?
5. What was Tina's pet peeve about Amanda Jo?
6. Tina decided to come up with her own magazine, why?
7. What are some of the things that contributed to Tina getting bad grades?
8. During her visit to Mrs. Simmons' class what did Tina's mother learn about Tina?

9. Why didn't Tina make the cheerleading squad in elementary?
10. What are some of the physical changes your body goes through during puberty?
11. Why was Tina upset when she saw Marci and Christopher Edwards hugging?
12. Why didn't Tina's mother allow Amanda Jo to sleepover? Do you think she overreacted? Why/Why Not?
13. Why did Tina steal Patrice's purse?
14. Why did Tina wait so late to tell Amanda Jo that she couldn't sleep over?
15. Amanda Jo wasn't missing she just failed to tell everyone that she was over Nancy's. Was Amanda Jo being responsible? Why/Why not?
16. What was Tina's reaction when she started her comma?
17. What did Tina like about Chante Baker?
18. Tina didn't like having a student planner. Why?
19. Why did Lauren want to be airbrushed for the cover of Bona Fide?
20. How did Tina realize that she changed?

Discussion Questions

1. Health Class was a time for Tina to let loose. Have you ever had a class that you weren't focused in? What type of things did you do?
2. Tina thought that if she wore makeup and carried a purse Christopher Edwards would like her more. Have you ever tried to change your appearance to get someone to like you?
3. Writing in a diary helped Tina express herself. How do you express yourself?
4. Chante Baker wrote a very unflattering note about Tina. Has anyone ever wrote a bad note about you? How did it make you feel?
5. How do you feel about the images of women in videos and magazines? Do these images bother you?

6. Sometimes when you're so focused on yourself you can forget about what's happening around you. Tina totally ignored the signs that her mother was pregnant. Have you ever ignored your parent(s) when something important was going on with them?
7. Sometimes when you're not focused in school there are other things going on in your life. How do you deal with your personal problems?
8. The Health Workshop was designed to help students talk about social issues that may be affecting them. Do you think it's a good idea to talk about your problems in an open forum with classmates and your teacher? Why/Why Not?
9. Tina and her sister Patrice argued a lot. What kind of relationship do you have with your sibling(s)? If you're the only child what kind of relationship do you have with your friends or cousins?
10. Starting your comma symbolizes that you're getting older. How do you feel about getting older and starting your comma? Are/were you scared, excited, nervous?

11. Sometimes parents say things that can sometimes hurt your feelings without realizing it. Tina over heard her mother call her foolish. Have your parents ever said something to you that hurt your feelings? How did you deal with this?
12. It's safe to say that Tina didn't want to share Marci with Nancy. Why do you think some friends are insecure about letting new friends inside the circle?

CPSIA information can be obtained at www.ICGtesting.com
Printed in the USA
LVOW080318040812

292871LV00001B/1/P

9 781432 740269